Flask (about songs and souls and things which live in bottles) and the National Theatre premiere of her play *Island* – on which this novel is based.

Nicky has three (pretty grown-up) children and lives with her husband in Brighton

also by Nicky Singer

FOR ADULTS

To Still the Child

To Have and To Hold

What She Wanted

My Mother's Daughter

FOR YOUNG PEOPLE

Feather Boy

Doll

The Innocent's Story

GemX

Knight Crew

The Flask

NON-FICTION

The Tiny Book of Time

(with Kim Pickin)

The Little Book of the Millennium

(with Jackie Singer)

STAGE

Feather Boy the Musical

(National Theatre; with Peter Tabern, Debbie Wiseman and Don Black)

Knight Crew

(Glyndebourne; with Julian Philips)

Island

(National Theatre)

ISLAND

NICKY SINGER

Illustrated by Chris Riddell

CABOODLE BOOKS LTD

Published by Caboodle Books Ltd 2015

A Catalogue record for this book is available from the British Library.

ISBN: 978-0-9929389-6-3

Typeset by CB editions, London
Cover design: www.spikyshooz.com
Printed and bound by CPI Group (UK) Ltd, Croydon, CR0 4YY

The paper and board used in this book are natural recyclable products made from wood grown in sustainable forests. The manufacturing processes conform to the environmental regulations of the country of origin.

Caboodle Books Ltd
Riversdale
8 Rivock Avenue
Steeton, BD20 6SA, UK

For Frances Rose

who taught me how to be 'awake for possibilities'

ISLAND

UKPIK

1

The island waited.

It was midnight but not dark. The sun was out. An Arctic summer sun that lit a pathway across the freezing water. The air shimmered. And in that shimmering air was the rhythmic beat of wings.

Ukpik was flying.

Ukpik, the owl with the yellow eyes and the snow-white feathers.

The tundra ghost, they called her. White against the glassy sea, white against the black sand of the beach. And white on the hill.

If she landed on the hill.

In times gone by, the island's hunters would have watched for that bird, tracked it as it came inland.

For *ukpik* on the hill – so the ancestors said – meant death.

But the hunters were long dead themselves, buried in the sacred ground, and only the sun looked down that night. So no one heard the beat of *ukpik*'s wings, or followed the yellow eyes and the snow-white feathers.

And no one saw where the great bird landed.

2

Three thousand, eight hundred and thirty-five miles south and east of the island, in a small London flat, Cameron O'Connor banged his fist on the kitchen table.

'No,' he said. 'No. No, NO!'

Dr Pascale O'Connor (research scientist, mother), watched her coffee mug jiggle. She watched her laptop jiggle. Her screensaver – which was a picture of the island – went up and down. 'Don't shout, Cameron,' she said.

'No way,' shouted Cameron. 'I am not going to Herschel Island. End of.'

'The trip's been booked for months,' his mother reminded him.

'So, cancel it!'

'Oh, right,' said Pascale. 'That'll just be the return flight from London to Calgary and the one from Calgary to Whitehorse and the one from Whitehorse to Inuvik and the one from Inuvik . . .' She paused. 'Cameron, we leave on Monday.'

'You leave on Monday,' said Cameron.

'Most boys your age would give their right arm for a week on an Arctic island,' Pascale mentioned.

There were many things Cameron might have said about that. He might have said: *Since when was I most boys?* Or, *have you forgotten it's Tom's birthday party on*

Thursday? Or, perhaps a little more accurately, *Not if they had to go with YOU!*

'Besides,' Pascale continued, 'you agreed.'

'Yes,' said Cameron. 'I fell for the Arctic bit. You know – snow and ice. I didn't realise that it was going to be,' he gestured at the green, hillocky land of her screensaver, 'just like Scotland.'

Pascale arched an eyebrow. She always conducted her climate research in the summer. For each of ten years, in fact, she'd made the annual trip in July, so the island was always 'just like Scotland'. He'd seen the photos and he wasn't stupid (well, not that stupid) and . . . She smiled sweetly. 'Well, since it was your dad who paid for the tickets and with whom you'll presumably be staying if you don't come, perhaps you'd better just run the new plan past him?'

'Obviously,' said Cameron, and his mouth set into a little line which made him, Pascale thought, look not unlike her ex-husband.

She closed her laptop. 'Cameron,' she said, 'what exactly do you think is going to happen on the island?'

'Nothing,' exploded Cameron. 'That's the point. A whole week of absolutely nothing!'

3

A hundred miles north of the island, the 2 a.m. sun threw long shadows across the pack-ice. Where the edge of the ice met the open sea, waves crashed and battered. Under the relentless pounding, ice broke away, floating in giant floes on the surface of the water. The floes moved with the swell of the ocean, pulled back and forth with the tides.

Or, at least, they should have done.

But there was one floe which was not moving in time with the rest. This huge disc of ice seemed to be being buffeted by some other force. It moved and trembled as if it was being pushed from below. As if some powerful thing was rising from a place deeper than the ocean itself.

If the ancestors had been watching (and the ancestors were always watching) they would have nodded to each other and said:

A spirit is walking.

Then they would have waited – patiently – to see what form that restless soul would take, and where it might be heading.

'*Pisugtoq,*' they would have murmured to each other when the creature finally broke the surface of the water. 'It is *pisugtoq*. The Ever-Wandering One.'

And then, as the creature twisted south: 'Ah. The island then. The spirit is going to the island.'

4

'So what changed, exactly, Cam?' Cameron's father's tone was light and business-like down the phone.

'Nothing,' said Cameron.

Hugh O'Connor waited.

'She told me about the power situation,' Cameron improvised.

'Power situation?'

'Electricity. Wi-fi. Phone signal. Or lack of.'

'Come on, Cam! Herschel Island is about as far north as you can go without bumping into the North Pole,' said his father. 'What exactly did you expect?'

Actually, Cameron had expected full power and possibly internet. Why not? His mother took her computer every year, didn't she? How was he to know that the tiny generator on the island was apparently marked For the Benefit of Science Only? And as for the phone signal – well, phone signals bounced off satellites, didn't they? Was Herschel in some parallel universe?

'I just want to stay with you,' said Cameron in a rush.

'Stay?'

'Yes.' There, he'd said it. 'With you.'

There was a pause. 'Look, Cam, flight costs aside – and to be frank that's quite a big aside – next week isn't brilliant timing for me.'

'It's Christine, isn't it?' His father's new girlfriend.

'Well, not just Chris, no.'

Just Chris, then. Just Chris!

'Only she doesn't have kids of her own, as you know, and it's early days and . . .' his father trailed off.

It had been like this since the divorce. For years he'd had to take second place. To them. His father's women. And there were so many women in the world. But a son only ever had one father. Couldn't his dad see that?

'Besides,' continued Hugh, 'your mum's wanted to take you to Herschel Island pretty much since you were born. And you've never been old enough. And now you're thirteen . . .'

Nearly fourteen, actually.

'I'd rather stay with you,' said Cameron solidly, wishing he could say that thing that could never be said. That thing that sounded so simple. *I love you, Dad.*

'You could take pictures,' said Hugh. 'Or make a video diary, maybe. Come down the weekend after you get back. Give Chris and me a show.'

'No vid-cam,' said Cameron.

'Well, I'm sure we could sort that,' said Hugh.

With money, Cameron thought. His father sorted a lot of things with money.

Silence.

'Look,' said Hugh, 'I know things haven't been too good between you and your mum recently, Cam, but, well – think of it maybe as quality mother and son time.'

And that, perhaps, was what was really frightening Cameron.

5

In the summer of the Arctic circle, the sun neither rises nor sets, so it's difficult to know when time passes. But time had passed and the creature from the north had almost reached its destination.

As it approached the island it looked not much more than a wave. And perhaps, in this moment, it was just a wave. For spirit creatures travel in many guises and one must be careful to assume nothing about shape and form. For shapes can change. Shift.

So here it was, then, this wave, one of the many waves that formed the ridge of water making its relentless way towards the shore. Nearer and nearer the wave came. And only the most watchful hunter would have seen the moment when, beneath the plume and spray, this wave gained muscle and sinew.

And also claws.

The creature did not fall upon the beach, it pounced and leapt there. Leaving, in the soft black soil, a mark. Four marks. Prints, the beginning of a track. The depth of the indentations would have told an island hunter that the creature must weigh at least seven hundred pounds. The heavy pads, the five distinctive toes and the non-retractable claw marks would all have said *pisugtoq* – the Ever-Wandering One. The slightly pigeon-toed gait would have given away her sex – female.

But the island's hunters were all in the sacred

PISUGTOQ

ground, so there was no one to see that day as the huge creature lumbered up the beach.

This sea-bear.

She-bear.

Spirit-bear.

The bear shook herself. In the Arctic summer sun the spray glittered from her coat. Against the shrub greens and browns of the tundra, she looked white. But her fur was actually flashed with apricot, gold, cream and straw yellow; the deeper tones of an older bear.

The bear stood still a moment, lifting her great snout to the wind. Her nostrils quivered with the fresh sweetness of her birthplace, the island's grasses, lichens, crowberries – and then it came, that sudden burning tang of jet fuel.

So, Atka the old she-bear thought, *I was right.*

She moved swiftly up the beach, picking her way between the strewn wood. There were single branches here and whole tree trunks. Wood which had been swept down the Mackenzie River, stripped white by the sea and then flung onto the shore like so many whale bones.

Within a few minutes the bear had gained sufficient ground to be able to see down to the inland side of the spit, where the makeshift runway was. The plane was already departing. Left behind on the ground were some boxes, some crates and two brightly coloured figures. One figure she recognised instantly. The woman who came every year. The woman whose mind she had tried – and failed – to reach so many times. The woman who saw nothing of the island, heard nothing of the island. The other figure was new to her. The bear focused her pin-prick dark eyes, waited until the slight figure turned, and the face became visible.

It was a child.

A child!

A child could change everything.

6

Cameron stood on the runway and watched the departure of the twin-engined airplane with a certain sense of disbelief. It seemed only a moment since he had emphatically refused to come to the island.

No way. I am not going to Herschel Island. End of!

Yet here he was.

Approximately three thousand, eight hundred and thirty-five miles from home. His final contact with civilisation (he was still staring upwards) getting smaller by the moment.

OK, so the departing twin-engined otter wasn't exactly the class of plane on which they had journeyed from London to Canada (decent food, uninterrupted multimedia) or even the one in which they'd made the trip from Calgary to Whitehorse (tolerably interesting trip to cockpit), it was just some howling tin bucket held together with rust and a prayer but at least it came with some life and some noise and a human being that wasn't his mother. And what was this marvellous contraption doing? Flying away, that's what: roar, boom, sputter.

Gone.

Even the vapour trail had almost vanished now. As though the plane had just been some mirage, and reality now consisted of this minuscule island in the middle of exactly nowhere. Herschel Island, to give it it's correct geographical name. With the emphasis on the 'her' bit. Her island.

'Oh look, Cameron!' his mother had screamed above the noise of the plane engine. 'There it is, can you see it?'

Did she think he was blind? Of course he could see it.

What there was of it.

This over-excitement of his mother's had begun when they'd first entered Canadian airspace.

'Why don't you just turn that thing off and look out the window?' she said. 'It's amazing. Look!'

Without turning the sound down on his film, he'd looked. There had been miles and miles of nothing: not a road, not a building, not a house, no habitation of any kind, in fact. Worse still, a whole hour's flying-time later – when she'd forced his nose against the window glass a second time – it had looked *precisely the same*. As though they weren't moving, or time had stood still. In every direction, as far as the eye could see, there it was again: this stretching nothingness. But at least it had been a big nothingness, big dark forests and big blue lakes and big white mountain tops. But here?

What was this island?

From the air it had been a tiny green dot. And now they'd arrived? It was a very slightly larger green dot. A green dot with a long mud beach attached. This beach which stuck out from the main island like some extra leg was actually, so his mother had been happy to inform him, a *spit*. Spit was about right. It was dirt. A long dirt beach with an inland bay one side and the Arctic Ocean the other, topped off (he briefly swung his head left and right) by some seriously weird tree trunks.

There was also – now the plane had gone – the silence.

Only not quite the silence. From somewhere near Cameron's face came a high-pitched whining noise. He slapped at his cheek.

'I don't believe it,' he exclaimed. 'An Arctic island. With mosquitoes!'

Dr Pascale O'Connor, who had her back to her son, did not reply. Dressed in a bright purple windcheater, her tall, athletic body was bent over sleeping bags, billy cans, data loggers and levelling rods.

Cameron looked back up into the sky as if he could make the plane reappear by force of will alone.

The heavens remained resolutely empty. The plane wouldn't be back for a week. A week! As the full horror of it hit him, he consoled himself with the thought of the gun.

Yes, that's what had persuaded him to come to the island.

She'd finally promised to let him have a go with her Wards Western Field bolt-action rifle.

7

I must go to the hill, the bear thought. *Find the stick.*

She set off along the ridge of the beach. There were shallow pools of sea water where the spit ended and the main body of the island began. From here, the land rose gently and the tundra grass was soft and hummocky underfoot. The blue Arctic lupins were in bloom.

The journey from the shore to the hill took less than half an hour. The bear could have walked blindfold across the summer tussocks and never lost her footing just as, when the winter snows came (and the land lost depth and horizon), she could find her way straight back to the frozen sea. She paused only once, when she thought she felt a pair of yellow eyes watching her. She turned, looking for the snowy feathers of *ukpik* the owl. But there was nothing behind her but the rustling of wind.

Reaching the brow of the hill was like coming home. The bear had denned here. Dug deep in the frozen peat to give birth to her young. She made straight for the old fox mound. The soil was fertile with fox scat and *aqpik* – the cloudberry rose – grew densely here, pushing its shy white petals above the low-lying green. Above the stick. For that's all it was, this thing which the bear sought, a small, straightish stick, or perhaps a staff, bleached by the sea and slightly thickened at one end, as if it had been selected to rest comfortably in the palm of a hand.

A human hand.

The bear curled a huge paw about the gnarled head of the stick and remembered. Remembered this sea-washed remnant as a white spruce growing young and straight in the Mackenzie delta. Felt the rise of its sap as if in her own veins. Smelt again its cool, heady, forest scent of pine. If you'd seen how the bear's great head bowed, you might have thought that she was giving thanks for this spruce, honouring the tree's life. Its particular, sacred spirit. Though perhaps she was also just watching how, as she held the staff (and actually it was a staff), the white fur of her paw retracted slightly, revealing dark and leathery skin.

It's always the fingers, she thought, which give you away first.

The fur at her back was contracting too, she felt it move, sloughed it slightly from her shoulders so it hung loose, like a garment chosen for protection rather than her own pelt and skin. At the same time, the weight of her body lessened and shifted, fell more upon her back legs as her posture became more upright. She looked down at her feet.

Such small feet.

How many thousand miles had these feet walked? How far wandered, swum, flown? Though encased in caribou and sealskin boots, as they now were, they looked no different from the feet of any other

Inuvialuit old woman. Atka waited, feeling her body begin to settle as the last traces of fur disappeared from her wrists.

She was animal no longer.

She had shifted. Changed once more.

She-bear had given way to She-woman.

An old woman with wrinkled skin and a heavy heart. For, despite the loss of so much body weight, Atka's mind remained burdened. When she was sure the transformation was finally complete, and even her claws were merely fingernails, Atka grasped the staff once more. Her mind was made up. She must wake Inuluk. There would be risks of course. But she had to take those risks. Because things had changed. Because of the youngster – the boy who had come in the aeroplane.

For why had the southern boy come – if not because Raven had willed it so?

Atka raised her right hand high and drove the staff down into the thin layer of soil at her feet. Drove it hard and fast, as though she needed to be able to feel the solidity of the ice beneath.

The ground shuddered. A small hummock at her feet shuddered. Trembled and woke. The child who had been curled there, no more or less than a piece of the green earth, woke.

The child rubbed her eyes, sat up slowly and wiped her face of dreams.

'Hello, Grandmother,' she said.

ATKA

8

Back on the beach, Dr Pascale O'Connor was still busy with the equipment. She was a strong woman (to get where she'd got in life, she'd had to be) and she was used to carrying a great deal of gear. Over the years she had devised precise and efficient ways of loading things about her body. But this was a trip for two and she seemed short of an arm for a tripod, a tarpaulin and a box of food tins.

'Cameron?'

No reply.

She looked up. Cameron had his iPod in. The iPod she'd politely asked him not to bring.

'It's pointless anyway. You won't be able to recharge it,' she'd told him.

But then Cameron's father had got involved.

'Look,' Hugh had said, in his most reasonable tone of voice, 'I know the island only has one generator.'

'A very small generator,' she'd put in.

'. . . but seriously, Pascale – how much energy can an iPod possible drain?'

What annoyed her most was the fact that the iPod wasn't really the issue. It was all about the Flipcam. The expensive 'little present' Hugh had given his son. And the fact that the camera needed to be recharged too.

'No,' said Pascale. 'No! Why do you always have to undermine me?'

'I just thought the camera might help,' Hugh had said smoothly, 'you know, help Cameron get into the trip more. Making a video film . . . Come on, Pascale. Be reasonable.'

She was a reasonable woman, a rational woman. She was a scientist. So she'd agreed (finally) to the iPod, she'd agreed (through gritted teeth) to the Flipcam.

'But absolutely no to your phone and no to your laptop,' she said. 'And that's final.'

The Flipcam and the iPod had both come hand luggage. Though, to be fair, she hadn't seen much of the Flipcam on the journey so far, in fact she'd begun to think it might be still in its unopened box on their return home and that would serve Hugh right. Not that he'd probably ever ask after the bit of gear again.

But the iPod.

The iPod! He'd brought the wretched thing to supper in Calgary, to breakfast in Whitehorse and now – within five minutes of landing on the island, there he was, plugged in again.

'Cameron!' Dr O'Connor shouted, gesturing mencingly at the items arranged at her feet.

Cameron jumped up onto one of the weird grey tree trunks. He smiled and he jigged. That was the point of an iPod, he always thought, it stopped you having to pay attention to other people.

Dr O'Connor put down various of the heavier items in her load and slipped her right hand inside the inner pocket of her windcheater. She withdrew a large steel whistle and blew it.

Very loudly.

Cameron pulled out the iPod. Did anyone in the world, he wondered, have a mother quite as irritating as his?

9

On the ridge of the hill, Atka looked at the child's upturned moon face, her seal-dark eyes.

'Feels as if I've been asleep forever,' the child said, yawning.

She was beautiful, Atka thought. Even now. What happened should never have happened. Atka put the thought away in a deep place.

'You never sleep, do you, Grandmother?'

'No. Not any more.' A child wiser than her years, then. Or perhaps just not a child after all. Inuluk was a girl, a girl on the brink of being a young woman. *How could I have forgotten that?*

Inuluk stretched and rearranged her *amouti* about her. The caribou-skin parka did not have a hood. Inuluk would never wear an *amouti* with a hood. The hood was for a baby and Inuluk would never carry a child of her own. Atka put that thought away too.

'So which lesson is it today?' asked Inuluk. 'Raven? The ancestors? The dreams? Or is it the fear?' She rose to her haunches, a little furrow in her brow. '*Kappia, irksi, ilira,*' she said, reciting the fear words in the language of her people. And then, as she turned to smile at her grandmother, her attention was caught by a sudden drift of cloudberry rose petals.

'It's summer,' she said, startled, and she jumped to her feet and looked about her. The tundra was green, the sea below them completely free of ice. 'You never wake me for lessons in the summer!'

'Things have changed,' said Atka.

'Changed?'

'The island cannot wait forever, Inuluk.'

'Is she here, then?' cried Inuluk. 'The *Qallunaat* – the white woman? The southerner? Is she here right now?'

'Yes,' said Atka.

'Then this isn't a lesson, Grandmother,' said Inuluk. 'Is it?'

'No,' said Atka.

'In the beginning was Raven,' Inuluk began in a rush. 'He made earth and soil, planted his world with lichen and pea-pods. Thousands of pea-pods . . .' she broke off. 'What if I forget things?'

'You won't,' said Atka.

'What if I don't know enough?'

'Everything my grandmother taught me, I have taught you,' Atka said.

'But what if the *Qallunaat* doesn't listen to me as she has never listened to you?'

'There is a young one come this time.' Atka pictured the small, brightly coloured figure on the landing strip. 'A child.' Atka paused. 'Like you.'

'Like me?'

'The soul of a child is not as fixed as that of grown man or woman,' Atka continued. 'You will concentrate on the child, Inuluk.'

'But –'

'Enough,' cried Atka. 'The future of the island – it is in your hands now.'

10

Cameron jumped down from the tree trunk, narrowly missing some grey driftwood branches which were jumbled together like a pile of old bones. 'And you brought that why?' he asked sweetly, nodding at his mother's silver whistle.

Dr O'Connor put the whistle back in her pocket. 'For the bears,' she said. 'Primarily.'

'Let me guess,' Cameron said. 'Dr Pascale O'Connor, previously known as my mother, gives up long-term permafrost study to teach bears how to referee.'

'Don't be stupid, Cameron. Bears are dangerous. If you can scare them, you don't have to shoot them.'

Bears interested Cameron. Almost as much as guns. 'Can I ask you a question?' he said.

'You can if you pick up that tarpaulin right there. And the box. And the tripod.'

'How far is it to the cabin?' Cameron said.

'Is that the question?'

'No it's not *the* question. It's just *a* question.'

'The cabin,' said Pascale, 'is considerably closer if you can take all the gear in one go, rather than have to make two journeys.'

'Ha ha,' said Cameron, hefting the box (which was flimsier than it looked and a great deal heavier) and the tripod. The legs of the tripod, which had only been on the ground a couple of minutes, seemed already to have taken on some of the dirt of the island. He could almost feel the grit beneath his fingernails.

'And if *the* question is why I'm allowed my computer here,' Pascale continued, 'and you're not . . .'

'Nope.' Cameron grabbed the tarpaulin. There was another small flurry of earth.

'OK,' she said. 'Fire away.'

'If it was me or the bear,' Cameron began, 'I mean massive bear, paws the size of dinner plates, four rows of razor-sharp teeth . . .' It was difficult doing the relevant gestures with your arms full of gear.

'They don't have four rows of teeth, Cameron, they have –'

'Okay. OKAY. Joke. You know – joke?' She didn't know. She had a sense of humour bypass. 'Anyway, this bear, this said huge bear has me in a headlock. I'm looking in its eyes.' His mother had already begun walking and he clanked after her, feeling his feet sink a little into the soft ground of the beach. 'Certain death,' Cameron added, catching up with her and putting himself in her direct eyeline. 'I mean, would you shoot or just blow the whistle?'

His gaze arrested her. Those very blue, very demanding eyes.

Just like his father's.

'Blow the whistle, probably, ' she said.

Cameron turned away. 'Thought so,' he said.

Idiot, she thought, I'm an idiot. How was it his fault that he looked like his father? But why did he always have to test her like this? And, more to the point, why did she always fail that test? It wasn't as if she couldn't see the small boy lurking just beneath the surface of the emerging young man.

'Don't worry,' she added quickly nodding at the gear draped around her body. 'I do have access to bells, fire crackers and bear spray.'

11

Atka guided Inuluk from the hill. Like wind over grass, the two of them glided and flew to a tundra ridge just above the place where the *Qallunaat* were unpacking. Framed against the shining inland bay and the wide blue arc of the sky, the figures on the beach seemed small and stupidly busy.

The old woman and her grandchild spent many minutes crouched in silence observing the *Qallunaat*, before Inuluk finally whispered: 'Is that really them, Grandmother?'

'Yes.'

'The people who change nature?'

'Yes,' replied Atka.

Inuluk looked again. The clothes the *Qallunaat* were wearing were strange – harshly bright and very thin, so they flapped around their bodies. Their skin was strange too, pale white, the colour of ghosts. But they had eyes and noses and hair. They walked. They talked.

'They don't look that dangerous,' she said.

Atka, meanwhile, had not once moved her gaze from the boy – yet it was not the boy she saw. For in that moment she had travelled to a different place. Was standing in the *kamiks* – the sealskin hunting boots – of Tuligaak, her father. Seeing what Tuligaak saw when the first white man stepped onto the island. Feeling

QALLUNAAT...

The white people of the South...

what he felt – a fresh fear, a terror. For in one hand the white demon had been carrying a metal knife and, in the other, a weapon Tuligaak had never seen before. When the demon lifted the never-before-seen weapon to his shoulder, its metal muzzle exploded with fire.

'When your great-grandfather saw the first white man . . .' began Atka.

'He began to sing,' interrupted Inuluk. 'To chant. He went into a trance, flew with *ukpik*, the snowy owl. Travelled in dreams. I know that, Grandmother.'

'And when he returned from his journey,' Atka continued, 'and the people asked what he had seen, he said –'

'The men from the ships will murder us,' quoted Inuluk.

'Yes. And no one believed him.'

'And then the killing started,' said Inuluk, dutifully.

'Yes.'

'But Grandmother – that was all so long ago!'

Atka rose, staff in hand. Inuluk followed her upward movement, saw the old woman outlined against the island. The flow and shape of her body seemed to mirror the hills and the hollows of the land behind.

'The summer is never so long,' said Atka, 'that you can forget the winter.'

12

'Bear spray?' said Cameron. His mother was ahead of him again, and he was toiling after her, watching his footing as they moved up the spit and the dirt beach gave way to random tufts of grass and denser scatterings of the bone-like bits of driftwood. 'Bear spray!'

'Yes,' said Pascale. 'Tins of. It works like a fire extinguisher. You pull the pin and spray at an oncoming bear. Easy to use and highly effective.'

'What about the gun?' said Cameron, dodging a stick that looked like a pair of antlers.

'The gun?'

'You did bring the gun, didn't you?'

'Of course I brought the gun, Cameron,' said Dr Pascale O'Connor.

The voices of the *Qallunaat* floated upwards towards the tundra mound where Atka still stood, staff in hand.

'You see?' Atka said. She watched the two figures proceed along the beach. They were heading in the general direction of a small cluster of dilapidated wooden huts first built by the Pacific Steam Whaling Company over a hundred years previously.

'It's only a conversation,' said Inuluk, stubbornly.

'You're young,' began Atka.

'Young!' Inuluk burst out. 'Sometime I feel a hundred years old. A thousand. Sometime I think you've filled my head so full of the past, I've lost sight of the future.'

In my day, Atka thought, a child would never interrupt an elder. And no one would ever interrupt a story. A storyteller could speak for hours and no one would say a word. 'There will be no future, Inuluk, unless you tell him. Tell him everything as I have taught it you.'

'Yes,' said Inuluk, obedient again. 'I will tell him the stories. The stories of our people. Teach him the lessons. So he will understand. Tell his own people. And then they'll stop melting our world. Lesson One: Raven. Lesson Two: the Ancestors. Lesson Three: the Dreams . . . He will listen, won't he grandmother?'

'I don't know,' said Atka. 'But, if not, there is always Lesson Four.'

'The Fear?' said Inuluk.

'Yes,' said Atka. 'The Fear.' And, very softly, as if she carried far more weight than an old woman had any right to, she began to pad across the cottongrass after the *Qallunaat*.

Dr O'Connor was walking along the tussocky ground as briskly as her load would allow. There was no need, she thought, for her to be so abrupt with her son. 'The problem with guns and bears, Cameron,' she said into his grumpy silence, 'is that shooting bears is expensive.' She made her tone light, gracious even. 'Only the local Inuvialuit population are allowed to harvest them, you see.'

'Harvest?' said Cameron, catching up with her. If anyone was following him, he wasn't aware of it. 'You *harvest* polar bears?'

'Yes. There's a quota. Take any more and you get fined. Take a bear if you're not a local and you get fined. Big money too.' Pascale paused. 'And – for the record – who said anything about polars? It's grizzlies we're more likely to find at this time of year. The polars – well, they should be back at sea by now.'

Somewhere behind her, behind Cameron (but not very far behind), came the sound of a low – polar – growl.

CAMERON

13

'This is it?' Cameron asked. His mother had stopped in front of what appeared to be a shack on the edge of a small abandoned village. No, *village* would be an exaggeration. It was more a cluster of random wooden dwellings. His mother's chosen hut was about double the size of a garden shed and painted white. Or had been painted white once. Now the paint was peeling from the wooden slats and the roof barely looked watertight. 'This is the *cabin*?'

'Count yourself lucky,' said Pascale. 'The first few years I came, I used to bring a tent. Go on, in you go. It's not locked.'

'Not locked?'

Pascale laughed. 'How many times do I have to tell you? Herschel is officially uninhabited now. Who would you lock a door against?'

Cameron used his tripod arm to push his way into a small ante-room. A space made smaller by the presence of a makeshift crate table, a couple of crate chairs, a Calor gas bottle and a camping stove.

Pascale put down her computer, her gun and the levelling rod and then inhaled deeply. 'I love the smell of this place,' she said.

Cameron sniffed. The place smelt of warm wood dust and salt, as though the cabin and all its contents had been drenched with sea-water and then left to dry out very slowly. It wasn't unpleasant, just a little musty, as though the air would always carry the memory of the soaking. It made Cameron wonder briefly about the history of the place. Who'd walked here and why? He didn't mention anything though because it would only mean some Bygone Days Lecture from his mother. But there was something else too. Cameron stood still a moment. The cabin had a strange air of *expectancy* (he couldn't think of a better word than this), as if it had been waiting for them. Or as if the cabin knew something about their time here that they didn't yet know?

Idiotic thought. Cameron shook it from him, dumped the tarpaulin (obliterating all floor space in the anteroom) and marched through to the back room. There was a window with flimsy curtains, a simple wooden wardrobe and one camp bed.

'Master bedroom,' he announced. 'So where are you sleeping then, Mother?'

Pascale, appearing behind him, pointed at the small piece of vacant floor next to the camp bed. 'In some similarly deluxe model approximately there.'

'You're joking,' said Cameron.

'No,' she opened the wardrobe to reveal green canvas. 'Yup, here's the spare.'

'Since when did *quality mother and son time* include having to share personal space?' Cameron burst out.

Pascale turned around. 'Who said we were having quality mother and son time?'

'Dad.'

'Oh. Typical. I suppose he told you to expect an en-suite bathroom too.'

'Where's the bathroom?' said Cameron.

'There isn't a bathroom, Cameron.'

'What about a loo?'

'There's the Throne Room, if that's what you mean.'

'The Throne Room?' said Cameron.

'Yes,' said his mother. 'That outside cubicle we passed. With the five steps leading up to it?' she added when he looked blank. 'We call it the Throne Room.'

'Outside?' said Cameron. 'The loo is *outside*?'

'Oh for heaven's sake, Cameron, grow up. This isn't the Ritz hotel. In fact, it isn't even a holiday. It's work. For me, anyway.'

'Everything's work for you,' said Cameron, the nakedness of the remark taking even him by surprise.

He had to get out, get away. Right now.

'I'm going to the Throne Room,' he announced.

14

Atka and Inuluk had followed the *Qallunaat* to the huts and watched them stow their luggage and close the cabin door behind them. So, Atka thought, we will have to wait until the morning to get the *Qallunaat* child alone. And she was prepared to wait.

She'd waited a hundred years, a thousand – so what was one more night?

But here the boy was, all of a sudden, exiting the cabin by himself. He was crossing towards the box on stilts.

Atka remembered when the *Qallunaat* had first constructed this box, positioning it alone in its landscape, its back to the inland bay, so that, from certain angles, it didn't look like a box at all, but a flat door. And she had wondered briefly, if this was how the white man thought to change realms: walk up a flight of five steps and open a door straight into the sky. That was before she understood the *Qallunaat* knew little about passing from earth to sky. Or earth to sea. Or earth to anywhere. Other realms, it seemed, did not interest them. This is what happened, she supposed, when you stopped being close to the animals.

'Come,' she said to Inuluk who was crouched down behind a particularly large pile of driftwood tree trunks.

But Inuluk didn't move. She had also been watching

the *Qallunaat*. 'Grandmother . . .' she said.

'Yes?' replied Atka.

'In all our talks, you never said that the task might involve, might be with . . .'

'Yes?' repeated Atka.

'. . . a boy.'

'Even Raven,' Atka said after a pause, 'doesn't know everything.'

15

The rickety door of the toilet was a surprisingly close fit. Very little light got in around the edges. But Cameron had seen enough before he closed the door. A plywood panel (with a hole cut in) suspended over what looked like a six-foot-deep ex-oil drum. The only other thing in the space was the gagging stench of the blue chemical liquid that swirled about beneath him.

He could do without light but not without air. He kicked the door open a bit with his heel. (Who, he reasoned, on this uninhabited island, was there to see him anyway?) But somehow the urge to perform had left him. He was about to exit when a thought struck him. If Hugh O'Connor wanted pictures of the trip then Hugh O'Connor would get then.

He reached into his trouser pocket and extracted the camera, flipped it open and pointed it at his face.

'Good evening, Father,' he said. 'I'd just like to show you what your money buys in this place.' Then he thrust the camera through the hole and into the stinking toilet tank. He waved it about.

'You'll note the interesting slurry formations – for which Mum could probably give you the correct Latin terms. Forms which will probably get more interesting as the week progresses,' he added.

Then he actually laughed. Maybe he had underestimated the fun he could have here.

He extracted the camera and, holding it at arm's length (just in case of contamination) pointed it back at his face.

'Meanwhile, Dad,' he added, 'you'll be interested to have an update on bears. Yes, that's bears. B, E , A, R, S – bears. My mother has a whistle. So if I get charged by a twelve-hundred-pound polar my mother, your wife – sorry, ex-wife – has let it be known that she will blow this whistle. Yes, Dad, that's blow a whistle, not fire a gun. So now you have full video evidence. Should I come home in a body bag, that is. Goodbye. Your soon to be dead son, Cameron.'

He flicked the thing off.

What next?

It seemed to him that he had two options:

Option 1: go back into the cabin where he'd never be more than ten foot from his mother.

Option 2: have himself some quality time out.

He descended the steps of the Throne Room, stepped on to the springy turf of the island and yelled: 'I'm going exploring!'

16

Pascale heard her son yell.

She contemplated opening the cabin door and yelling back: *Do you think you could just help with a little bit of unpacking first?*

But she didn't do that. Hadn't exploring been exactly what she'd been hoping Cameron would do? OK, so she'd hoped he might accompany her, that she might be able to show him something of her life's work, but wasn't this a start? Albeit one rather late in the day.

She opened the door.

'Terrific,' she said. 'But don't be long. And stay close to the cabin. Just in case –'

'Of the BEARS!' Cameron said, doing jazz hands and wide bear teeth. Then he turned, smiled and, while his mother was still watching, plugged in his iPod.

17

The conversation in the box on stilts had been too muffled for Inuluk to hear but she was close enough, behind her pile of driftwood, to see the boy unspool two long, thin white worms from his jacket pocket and attach one to each ear. The worms seemed to alter the boy's body language. She watched transfixed as he began to jerk his way along the shoreline towards the broader end of the spit where it joined the main part of the island.

'Follow him,' Atka instructed.

Inuluk followed him. Soon she'd caught up sufficiently to be able to hear the series of strange sounds that were coming out of the boy's mouth. She listened carefully. At first she thought it might be a tune but it wasn't very musical. The words sounded a bit like this:

'Mm . . . mm . . . mm . . . mm . . . mm . . . Madness!'

To these sounds the boy added a variety of apparently random movements: he punched the air, picked up a stick and banged it on a tree trunk, flicked his left wrist repeatedly across his stomach as if he had an itch there.

'Finally . . . finally . . . FINALLY. Hoo . . . ha . . . ha . . . HOO!'

The singing (if it was singing) and the movements continued as he walked further inland.

'Wah . . . wah . . . wah . . . I realised . . . realised . . . seen the light.'

'He's seen the light,' Inuluk whispered.

'You have to speak to him,' said Atka. 'Lesson One: Raven. Begin now.'

'Speak to him?' said Inuluk. 'But Grandmother – I think he's trancing.' And she was just wondering what sort of birds white people flew with in their dreams when the boy suddenly flung himself to the ground, his back flat to a small patch of grass as though he intended to sleep. Certainly he had his eyes shut – but his body continued to pump and jerk around on the ground.

'Is it real?' he shouted. *'Is it REAL!'*

Then – just as suddenly – he ripped the worms out of his ears and jumped right up again. Inuluk had rarely seen someone move so fast.

'Bored,' he exclaimed. 'Bored, bored, bored.'

Inuluk, not knowing what he might do next, took a very big step backwards.

18

'Thursday,' Cameron exclaimed aloud, getting himself a sudden idea. But was it Thursday? He counted carefully on his fingers, counted again. Somehow, he lost track of the days. Well, it was probably Thursday. Tom's birthday. Party time!

He got out the Flipcam again.

'Good evening, Bro,' he said, to the screen.

Atka immediately nudged Inuluk, as though 'Good evening, Bro' was some sort of introduction, the opening Inuluk required to start a conversation with the *Qallunaat*, even though it was clear that the boy was speaking to his gadget. But Atka, who had waited so long and was not impatient, had to know, had to know if she was right about the child.

Would the boy be able to see her granddaughter?

Would he be able to hear her?

Then Atka remembered with all the vividness of a dream the times – the so many times – that she, Atka, had been ignored by the *Qallunaat*. By the tourists, the oil men, the scientists. By the woman in the flimsy bright clothing who came every year, the woman who was obviously this boy's mother. All of them deaf to her voice, blind to her presence. No matter how loudly or softly she'd tried to tell the stories. Whether she had been wind or waves, land or bear, woman or spirit, to the *Qallunaat*, she – Atka, Guardian of the island –

was invisible. She did not exist.

Please, Atka whispered to Raven. *I beg you. Let the boy's soul not be fixed yet. Let him be able to see Inuluk. Hear her.*

And perhaps it was the force of this prayer that gave Inuluk what she experienced as a shove in the small of her back.

Cameron, meanwhile, was thinking. *Forget the family movie.* He would be loading to YouTube!

'This is Cameron O'Connor,' continued Cameron, 'reporting from beyond the known universe.' He thought his American accent was rather good. 'And Tom,' he added, with an affectionate tilt of his head at the mention of his best friend, 'if you're tuning in tonight, it's not that I've forgotten your birthday, buddy, it's just that I'm on Planet Yukon, approximately two million Canadian miles from yours. So I'm going to be' – he paused – 'late.'

He was good at this stuff. Maybe he'd get a hundred thousand hits and be able to charge for advertising.

'What intergalactic mission brings me here?' he continued. 'Global warming, my friend.' And quite suddenly, he turned on his heels and started walking directly towards the sea on the inland bay side of the spit.

'Quick,' said Atka, and Inuluk found herself bundled after him.

'See this,' said Cameron, waving the camera at the twilight blue water. 'This, believe it or not, is the Arctic

Ocean. No kidding, Tom, and this' – he zoomed in for a close-up – 'is a wave. Yes, Tom – a *wave*. And – due to the ongoing melting of the icecaps – there are apparently a lot more *waves* round here of a year than there used to be. I knew you'd be fascinated. Tell you what, I could be the first to bottle Genuine Unfrozen Arctic Water. Bring you home a sample for your birthday gift.'

It was at this moment that a second wave, rather larger than the one he was filming, washed up the beach. The water poured over Cameron's feet.

'Oh what! You're kidding me!' Cameron exclaimed. Then he pulled immediate focus on the camera and angled a shot down at his drenched trainers.

'Nature fights back,' he observed.

But nature never fought back, Atka thought. Nature endured and that was the problem.

Cameron zoomed in for a second close-up. Perhaps he could send the clip to the makers of *You've Been Framed*, make himself a quick fifty quid?

'Inuluk,' said Atka. 'You will speak. You must speak.'

But only Cameron spoke. 'Right, that's it,' he said as he squelched back up the beach. 'I think I'm done with the sun, sea and surf. Next up – Big Game Hunting.'

He turned his back on the sea and, picking up a stick and holding it at waist level like a gun, he strode purposefully up the spit towards the very green tussock where Inuluk and Atka were standing.

19

'I'm going on a bear hunt,' Cameron announced, swinging the gun stick left and right. One advantage of an uninhabited island – you could say whatever you wanted as loudly as you wanted.

Inuluk dropped to the earth.

She is afraid, Atka thought suddenly. *Inuluk is afraid!*

Atka watched the boy's advance. His . . . onslaught. What if he was too much for her granddaughter? Too bullying? Too idiotic? Or simply too closed? It was one thing to expect an Inuvialuit child to vibrate with her surroundings, but this boy? Schooled in the south? Perhaps his heart would never open. Perhaps he could never imagine himself more than he was – a thing of flesh and blood and limits. Then Inuluk would fail as surely as Atka herself had failed.

On the other hand, why had the *Qallunaat* woman brought the boy this year of all years? At a time when Inuluk's education was so nearly complete? The meeting must have been meant to be. Yes, Atka had to believe. She had to keep the faith. This was the way of the Guardians.

She felt her heart beat a little faster.

Crouched down, Inuluk was camouflaged against the earth in her caribou skins of brown, but still, she was quite plain to see, if you had been looking.

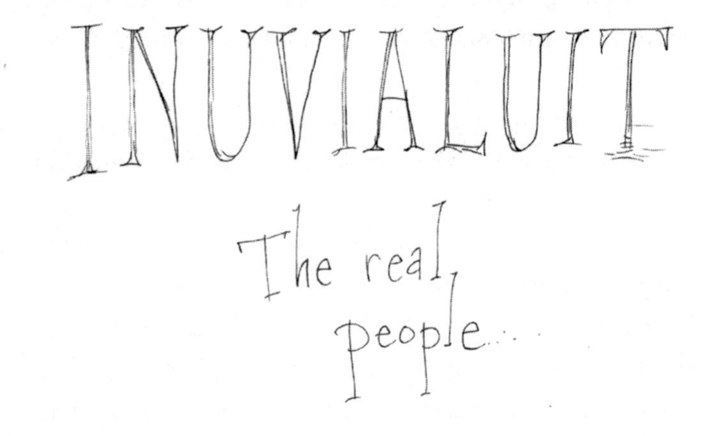
INUVIALUIT
The real people...

Cameron was not looking. He was waving his stick gun and shouting the words of his one-time favourite childhood bedtime story. The one his father (yes – his father!) used to read him when he was about four: 'Going on a Bear Hunt'. '*Gonna catch a big one! Swishy-swashy through the – hummocky – grass. I'm not scared!*'

He was almost upon them and still – nothing.

The moment was about to pass. The boy would walk blindly past Inuluk as all the *Qallunaat* had walked blindly past Atka. This could not be.

It could not!

Atka lifted her bleached wood staff and banged it into the earth.

For a second time that day the ground trembled. Inuluk trembled. And perhaps it was the movement of her body, the slight sway of her *amouti*, that finally caught Cameron's eye.

He came to a dead stop.

Squatting not a foot from him was a crouched figure. A figure, what's more, which appeared – beneath some wild fur-skin costume – to be a girl.

A girl!

The sheer, hideous embarrassment of it. How long had she been there? What had she heard? As for uninhabited island – one thing was certain, he was going to kill his mother.

Meanwhile – no time to lose. He dropped the stick, strode up to the girl, stretched out his hand and said:

'Hi, my name's Cameron.'

Atka's heart nearly burst then. *He sees you, Inuluk! He can see you!*

Inuluk heard those mind-speak words, heard them as clearly as if her grandmother had spoken aloud. And she should have felt the same joy but her heart recoiled.

Cameron, his hand still suspended mid-air, saw the look of terror in the girl's dark eyes. For heaven's sake. What did she think he was? A ghost? An alien? He withdrew his hand, watched while the girl steadied herself. Soon she was holding herself so still, she seemed to disappear into the landscape again.

For a moment Cameron stood nonplussed. Then he knelt down beside her and he flipped open the camera. 'What have we here?' he said in a gruff whisper, David Attenborough style. 'It's one of earth's most timid creatures. Some specimens have been known to have grass grow over them, they sit so still. Which is where it got its name – the Lesser-Known Arctic Hummock. Part animal. Part soil.'

He thought the girl might laugh. But she didn't, though her eyes were on him again. He'd never really seen eyes like that before – fierce and shy at the same time.

'OK – I get it,' he said. 'You don't speak English, do you?'

No reply.

'Sprechen sie – English?'

No reply.
'Parlez-vous ENGLISH?'
'My name,' said the girl, 'is Inuluk.'

INULUK

20

'Whoa!' said Cameron. 'Why didn't you say something before?'

'Because you were saying things,' the girl said simply.

Qallunaat – people without ears! People who speak but never listen! But even the anger couldn't mask Atka's exhilaration. *He can hear you, Inuluk. See you and hear you!*

'So what's with the crouching?' asked Cameron, wondering whether he could sit back on his heels the way the girl was doing and not lose his balance. It looked like some weird sort of Arctic yoga.

'*Quinuituq*,' Inuluk said.

'Good start,' said Atka, aloud this time. For could it be – could it be, this time, that she, Atka, would also be heard?

Inuluk turned naturally towards her grandmother as she spoke, but the boy did not. Not even when Atka moved, stood directly in his eyeline.

'Boy,' Atka called. 'BOY!'

But he remained focused on Inuluk. And, of course, that was what Atka had prayed for, longed for. But it didn't stop Atka feeling a sudden stab of disappointment that she herself remained invisible to him. The boy couldn't see her, or hear her, any more than the other *Qallunaats* had ever been able to see or hear her. No matter. No matter, she scolded herself. She would stand beside – behind – her granddaughter every step of the way. Together they would be heard.

'Quini-what?' said Cameron.

'Deep patience,' said Inuluk.

Cameron checked the girl's face to see if she was joking. She wasn't. 'Well I guess you'd need that in a place like Herschel Island,' he said.

Qikiqtaruk. Tell him, Inuluk.

'Qikiqtaruk,' said Inuluk.

'Okay . . .' said Cameron, and something made him do a little dance in front of her. 'It's a song?' He gave his best charades impression. 'It's . . . a film? It's' – he gave her a low mandarin bow, hands together in prayer – 'even deeper patience.'

'Our name for the island,' Inuluk said. 'Qikiqtaruk.'

'Meaning?'

'Island.'

'Inspired.' He grinned. 'Know what? I'd stick with Herschel, if I were you. More of a ring to it. Plus it gives you a clue about the bloke who discovered this place. He was British, John Herschel. Did you know that? Although it wasn't Herschel himself who came here but his mate Sir John Franklin who –' He stopped himself right there. Was he turning into his mother?

'No one discovered this island,' said Atka, aloud. She couldn't help herself. Some things needed to be spoken aloud. 'It was here already. It's always been here.'

QUINUITUQ
Deep patience...

And all at once Atka was back at her father's knee, listening to his long-ago voice. 'The *Qallunaat* have a word,' Tuligaak had said. 'It is this word: *own, to own*.' 'What does it mean?' she had asked. 'To possess,' her father had told her. 'To possess something that is yours only.' She remembered the question mark in his voice, as he tried to understand a society which had a word for something beyond sharing. There'd been a long silence and then he'd added, 'May there never be such a word in our language, Atka.'

'Our ancestors,' said Inuluk, 'my ancestors' – she corrected herself, as she remembered the boy couldn't see Atka – 'they lived here a thousand years before the first white man came.' Grandmother was right. The boy needed to learn. He needed to be respectful.

'Well, I guess the ancestors should have advertised themselves better then,' said Cameron. 'Put themselves on the map. I mean no one thought London was uninhabited and rocked up and planted a flag there, did they?'

'London?' queried Inuluk.

'Yes, London.' The girl looked totally blank. 'You must have heard of London?'

Don't go there. The mind-thought was sudden as Atka realised – with alarm – that paths always lead in two directions. What if, in trying to capture the soul of the boy, she lost the soul of her own granddaughter?

Don't go there, Inuluk. Don't go – even in a dream.

21

'As in London?' Cameron repeated. 'You know – LONDON?' He said it very loudly as though that alone would make her understand. 'Capital of Great Britain. Capital of the world, pretty much. Huge city. Massive. Millions of people. Activity. Excitement. Cars. Street lights. Street for that matter. Nice bit of concrete. Underground –'

'Under ground?' said Inuluk, whose mind found *tiriganniaq,* the tunnelling Arctic fox.

'Trains,' said Cameron, 'under the ground. And, above the ground, skyscrapers.' He pointed upwards.

'Sky scrapers?' repeated Inuluk, following his finger heavenwards.

'Giant buildings, taller than this island is wide, so tall they . . . scrape the sky. Well, bit of an exaggeration maybe. But you know, everything big, really big. London. Happening place.'

Atka saw something new in the boy then, something that she recognised: a fierce connection, a pride, a love of his homeland. His eyes were so brightly lit as he spoke that she could see right through to the place of his thoughts. This was the place she'd tried so often to reach with his mother. But the *Qallunaat* woman's eyes were like black stones, hard and ungiving. Atka felt her heart tremor and, against all of her instincts, her own better judgement, she let her mind loosen, freed her spirit to travel (it would only be for a moment, she told herself) into the open, excited eyes of the boy.

What she saw was beyond imagination.

The boy lived, it seemed, in a place without green.

Without grass.

Without soil.

Right up to the horizons in his land there was nothing but grey – glass, stone, metal. The buildings rose, just as he said, high into the sky like vertical sheets of ice. They reflected each other, hundreds of thousands of repeating squares and angles. In between the buildings was noise. Constant, screaming noise. People, machines, engines: roaring, yowling, coughing, choking. As if his world had forgotten how to be quiet, forgotten the grace of silence.

You would go mad in such a land, surely?

No wonder the *Qallunaat* were a jangling race.

She watched his people move, hundreds of them, swirling en masse, like herds of caribou between the pressing buildings. So many, many people. Where were they all galloping to? What new pastures did they seek? She couldn't see where they were heading, because the lights of the place flashed and blinded her: streams of red and yellow, punching pinks, throbbing greens. She felt herself folding, crumpling to the tundra grass, breathless, exhausted.

Inuluk did not witness the fall of her grandmother, her eyes were still on the boy.

'You must have seen it on the telly,' Cameron was saying, and then he stopped himself. 'Oh no – I forgot. You don't have telly, just like you don't have internet connection, because you don't actually have electricity. How do you people *live*?'

'You have connection,' said Inuluk suddenly.

'I'm sorry?'

'With Bro.'

'Bro?'

'And Tom. You can speak straight to – Tom.'

So she had heard him. He'd laugh if it wasn't so totally excruciating. She had heard everything! 'I was pretending,' he said quickly. 'You know – pretending? As in when you make stuff up?' Surely he wasn't going to have to explain make-believe as well as London? 'Tell me you know the difference between something that's real and something that's imagined?'

The girl said nothing.

'Mind you,' continued Cameron, 'my mother said you weren't real. She said this was an uninhabited island. So maybe you don't exist either. That could explain things.'

'Are the ear worms pretend?' asked Inuluk.

'The what?'

'The white worms you put in your ears that make sounds come out of your mouth?'

Now Cameron did laugh, laughed out loud. He couldn't help it. 'You mean my earphones. And they don't – oh forget it.' He pulled his iPod out of his pocket. 'Here – do you want a listen?'

And Atka, still on the ground, saw her granddaughter reach towards the boy. This was not how she had planned things. Not how she had planned things at all.

22

Inuluk took the worm that the boy held out to her. She saw that its head was like a large, white grub. She tentatively brought it towards her ear.

'In,' said Cameron, 'actually put it in.'

If he was happy to have large white grubs in his ear, what was there to be afraid of? She did as he asked. The shock was immediate, her head cracked and crackled with sound, a thousand different twangs in her skull. She pulled the thing out.

Which made the noise spill over, pulse out into the Arctic air. Atka, who was trying to get up, was battered down again. It's like the noise of his land, she thought, only balled up small. The sounds buzzed and fizzed and spat at her.

But Inuluk was reaching again for the grub head, placing it back in her ear. She listened with ever widening eyes.

'What is it?' she asked.

Fever. Atka was still on the earth. *Delirium.*

'Music, Inuluk. Progress. Civilisation.' Cameron snapped the iPod off. 'But I have to ration it, Herschel not exactly being on the national grid.'

The silencing of the machine brought Atka immediate relief. She felt herself rise as if a load had been taken from her shoulders, her mind. She was clear again. As she stood, stood at last, she was suddenly aware (above her, beyond her) of the snapping of wings. She knew those wings, the powerful way they rode the currents. She looked up. So – she'd been right after all. There had been yellow eyes on her back. *Ukpik*, the snowy owl, was flying. She glanced towards the hill. But the bird was not heading towards the hill.

Not yet.

But it was a sign. *Ukpik* was always a sign. *Ukpik* on the hill means death.

There was no time to waste.

Ask him why he's come.

'Why have you come?' Inuluk asked.

'Good question,' Cameron replied. 'And not one that has an easy answer. It has to do with two things, my mother and the fact that this island has no bedrock. This is a bedrock-free island. You're just living on a pile of earth. Sod. Soil. Did you know that?'

Atka knew that. She'd known for a millennia, from when the ice had stretched 3,000 miles south of the frozen ocean. An ice sheet which had ground and moaned its way across the continent, pushing soil out to its edges. Soil in the north which (when the ice finally retreated) became a crest of land. Qikiqtaruk. Her land. It was an ice age ago, but not something to forget.

'In fact, this whole island is just one of Mother Nature's accidents, apparently,' Cameron added.

'Gaia has no accidents,' cried Atka aloud. Not that Cameron heard her.

'Truth is, there's nothing holding you together,' Cameron continued, 'except ice. Well, permafrost anyway. And that's melting. My mum's measuring just how long it's going to take you to slip right into the sea.'

'The island,' cried Inuluk, 'the whole island – it will just wash away?'

So, thought Atka, she never really believed me then. Perhaps this would urge her granddaughter to the task.

'Got it in one,' said Cameron.

Haven't I told you a thousand times? It's just as it was before. The Qallunaat, they destroy with no thought of what – or who – they destroy.

'But no need to worry,' continued Cameron. 'According to Mum this global warming stuff is a centimetre by centimetre thing. So you've got a bit of time yet. And speaking of Mum, I'd better be getting back. See you tomorrow maybe? I mean, if you're not too busy with the – sitting.'

And he just turned and walked away.

23

Inuluk watched until the boy passed out of sight beyond the first of the huts. Watched his black hair. His jaunty gait.

'He spoke to me,' she said.

'A boy who leaks noise,' Atka said, hearing the anger in her voice. 'Even when he is alone, he cannot be quiet. He just talks. And talks.' To be angry was acceptable for a child but not for an adult. It was a failure of *isuma,* the capacity for sense and reason. But this boy – this boy!

'Spoke as if I was a real person again,' Inuluk continued. She turned her hands over and over in wonder. 'Real hands,' she said. 'Real feet.' She touched her face. 'Real face.'

'Buildings so high they almost touch the sky!' Atka exclaimed.

'I liked his iPod,' said Inuluk. 'Raven should have made iPod as well as pea-pod.'

'Who makes buildings, Inuluk, to block the sky?'

Inuluk turned to face the old woman. 'Cliffs, Grandmother. Perhaps they're only like cliffs?'

'Only birds live on cliffs,' said Atka.

'Well, he did fly here,' said Inuluk. 'So maybe he is a bird, a kind of Raven?'

'No! Never! He's a boy. A boy who laughs as he melts our world. Laughs as he blocks the sun and drills the

ISUMA
The capacity
for sense and reason
that comes
with
adulthood...

earth and washes our lives into the sea!' She paused, to catch her breath, to recover herself. 'Have you ever known such a boy, Inuluk?'

Inuluk stared back into the space that had been Cameron. 'No,' she said, 'I have never known such a boy.'

24

Cameron arrived in the cabin to find his mother firing up the camp stove.

'Oh, there you are,' Pascale said. 'I was beginning to get worried.' She blew out the match. 'So – did you spot anything interesting?'

'What's that?' said Cameron, pointing at some yellow gloop in a saucepan.

'That,' said Pascale, 'is your gourmet four-course dinner.'

'It's macaroni cheese,' said Cameron.

'Actually,' said Pascale, 'it's Kraft Dinner.'

'I hate macaroni cheese.'

'When in Rome, Cameron . . .' said Pascale, genially. 'Kraft Dinner is virtually Canada's national dish,' she added, stirring with a wooden spoon. 'Which is lucky because option two would probably be caribou stew. And I'm not sure you'd like that any better. And, speaking of caribou, did you see any, Cameron?'

'No. Should I have done?'

'Well, there are approx 169,000 animals in the Porcupine caribou herd and Herschel's really rich in *eriophorum* – the cottongrass they eat. So they do come here – I thought I told you that already?'

'Yeah. I think you just might have done.'

'OK. So, what animals did you see?'

'I didn't see any animals.'

'No?'

'No.'

'Birds?'

'No.' She'd given him lists, he remembered then. Animals, flowers, birds. Loads of bird. *Guillemots. Golden Plovers, Semipalmated Plovers, Red-Throated Loons, Pacific Loons. Common Loons.* Loony-bin loons! She'd thrust the lists into his pockets as if he was some kid going to I-spy camp.

'Were you looking, Cameron?'

'Of course I was looking, Mother.'

'So – what did you see?'

'Something much more interesting,' said Cameron. 'And rare. So rare as to be almost extinct, in fact.'

'Oh?'

'A girl.

'A girl?' Pascale looked genuinely surprised.

'That's right. On this *formally uninhabited* island I saw a girl.'

'What sort of girl?' Pascale said, ignoring his sarcasm.

'You know – arms, legs, head, that sort of thing.'

'Cameron –'

'About my age,' Cameron conceded. 'Or maybe a bit younger. Name of Inuluk.'

'Inuluk? Inuvialuit then. But there aren't any Inuvialuit on the island any more. Not living here anyway. Even the park rangers are only here a few months a year.'

'That's what I said,' said Cameron. 'You – I said – are a figment of my imagination.'

Pascale got out a couple of bowls and spooned in the bright yellow pasta. 'I suppose she could have been on the generational project.'

'The what?'

'The generational project,' Pascale repeated, handing him a bowl and a spoon. 'Sometimes elders take a boat from the mainland, bring children here, grandchildren, teach them about their heritage.'

'Because why?'

'Because it's all dying out. Their language. Their way of life. Sad, really. Right.' Pascale consulted her watch. 'Eat up. We're way late with this.' Cameron smelled the gloop. It didn't really smell of cheese or pasta. But he was, he realised, really quite hungry. He dug in.

'It's straight to bed after this,' Pascale continued.

'Bed?' said Cameron said. 'But it's still light!'

'It's 11.15 p.m.,' said Pascale. 'And, for the record, it's going to be light all night.'

'What?'

'You don't listen to a word I say, do you? In the summer here,' Pascale continued rather slowly, 'there is twenty-four-hour daylight . . . because . . .' She paused expectantly. 'Because of?' But Cameron wasn't playing. 'The tilt of the earth,' she finished.

'A place where is doesn't get dark?' said Cameron suddenly. 'That could seriously damage your brain. I mean that's what they do for torture, isn't it? In police cells. When they want you to talk. Keep the light on.'

'You don't have any problem with talking, Cameron.'

Cameron jumped up and opened the cabin door. She was right, of course. If it was late, it certainly didn't look late. It was (now he was paying attention), bizarrely, eerily light. 'And anyway,' he said, slightly desperate, 'I'm not tired. I'm not tired at all.'

And that reminded Pascale of how, the first time she'd ever come to the island, she'd sometimes stayed up all night. Had still been walking the bluffs or photographing soil slumps at four in the morning. Because time did seem to stretch here and different things felt important.

'OK,' said Pascale. 'Maybe there is time for a game of cards.'

'I rather have a go with the gun,' said Cameron.

25

A little way downwind of the cabin, Inuluk and her grandmother were sitting together on the hummocky ground.

'We do not know how long he will be here, Inuluk,' said Atka. 'You must start again. Try harder.'

'But Grandmother – it's difficult to tell him anything. There is no space between his words.'

'Then you must make space,' said Atka. 'Be more direct. I will help you. Tomorrow, we will begin at the beginning: Lesson One: Raven . . .'

'Man is not the most important part of creation . . .' began Inuluk obediently, but she was silenced by the sudden appearance of the *Qallunaat* woman from the cabin. Slung over her back was a gun.

Never could wait, my son, thought Pascale, as Cameron followed her out of the cabin with a box of ammunition. It reminded her of when he had been six months old and he'd wanted to walk before he'd even mastered crawling. He'd been so determined, so insistent, that somehow she'd spent her weekends bent double, supporting him under the armpits so that he could maintain the illusion that he could walk when, actually, he couldn't. She hadn't said 'no' to him then just as she hadn't said 'no' to him tonight. Maybe that was the root of the problem, being a firm person who'd never been quite firm enough with Cameron? Why hadn't she just said: *No, Cameron. It's too late. We'll get the gun out tomorrow*?

Instead, even though she still needed to run a final check on the gear she needed for slump-measuring and data-logging the following morning, she'd said: 'OK, Cameron. Why not?'

Well – nobody could say she wasn't trying.

Cameron looked at the gun in his mother's hands. It looked smaller than he remembered.

'It doesn't have a sight,' he said, disappointed.

'Of course it has a sight,' Pascale said, pointing at a small screw right at the end of the muzzle.

'That's a sight?' said Cameron. 'I meant a proper one. One of those telescopic things, so you can see what you're actually shooting at.'

'You use your eyes for that,' she said, drily. Adding, 'Not all guns look like the ones on your Xbox, you know.' Sometimes she thought he spent so much time in the virtual world he had no idea about real life at all. But perhaps it was just her, her being defensive about this .22 rifle that her father had given her when she was just twelve. Yes, she'd been twelve. Pascale fingered the smooth wood of the stock. Her mother had been shocked: 'What would you give a girl a gun for?' 'For rabbits,' said her father. But Pascale, an only child, knew it wasn't for rabbits. It was for bonding, father and daughter. Two years later, her father had died. And she held the gun, kept the gun (against her mother's better judgement) through all the years. In her twenties, she'd even taken lessons again. 'You're a natural,' her instructor had said, 'got a great eye.' And of course she'd liked the targets, liked being the best. But it wasn't just about that, it was about remembering, honouring the bond. Parent and child. So she'd always intended to teach Cameron to shoot. But somehow, there'd never been quite enough time. Or perhaps, she thought now, she just hadn't ever made that time?

'Can I have it, then?' Cameron asked, reaching.

'No,' said Pascale. 'Not yet.' She showed him the safety catch. She showed him how not to put his hands over the muzzle as he loaded the tubular magazine. She showed him how it took two pulls on the bolt to actually put a bullet in the chamber. She demonstrated how to bulwark the gunstock against his shoulder. 'OK,' she said finally, checking the safety for the tenth time, 'we're almost there.'

'It should be a Coke can,' Cameron said, positioning a Carnation milk tin on one of the dead tree trunks. 'A full can. When you hit a full Coke can, it explodes. I saw it on YouTube.'

'*If* you hit it,' said his mother.

Cameron held out his hands. 'Please?' he said.

And she gave him the gun.

It was heavier than he expected, now she wasn't clinging on to it, holding half its weight. He let off the safety, as instructed and positioned the butt against his shoulder.

'Careful now,' she couldn't help saying.

But he was being careful. He narrowed his eyes against the light and focused on getting the screw (which seemed tiny) on the 'o' of evaporated milk. He tried to hold still. His finger was on the trigger.

Bang!

The can pinged, wobbled and fell off the log.

'Bazinga!' shouted Cameron.

A slug of thick white milk flowed into the grass.

'First time. First time! Did you see that!' He turned to her, eyes shining.

'First time lucky,' she said. Which is what her father had said when she had downed a similar can, her first ever time.

'Why don't we go hunting?' he said. 'We could go tomorrow. Shoot some real stuff.'

'Hang on, hang on,' Pascale said.

'We could find a fox. Or caribou maybe. Get us some stew mix.'

'I told you, only the Inuvialuit can shoot game here.'

'OK, so we'd have to bring Inuluk with us. She could be our alibi. Either that or I have to find myself a bear.'

'A bear?' said Pascale 'That's the same difference,

legally speaking. Only the fine's bigger. About £2,000.'

'Well, the bear would have to find me then,' said Cameron, shouting over his shoulder as he went to set up the milk can again, only slightly further away this time. 'Then it'd be self-defence, right?'

He looked so happy, she thought.

'Right,' he said, returning and setting himself up again. 'Round two.' Then he paused. 'Would this gun really kill a bear?' he asked.

'So I have to hope,' said Pascale.

'I mean, the bullets seem tiny.'

'It's not about bullet size, it's about accuracy.'

'Really? Can't help thinking you'd be better off with a pump-action shotgun.'

'A bear can charge at 30 miles an hour, that's 14.33 yards a second –'

Oh, here we go, thought Cameron.

'– which means,' continued Pascale, 'that it can cover 50 yards in 3.4 seconds. Allowing for reaction time, even a very fast shooter can barely get in two shots in that time. Pump action more of course, but pump actions can jam. So it really comes down to accuracy, as I said, and that's easier with a gun you know well. If you're only going to have a couple of shots max, they'd better be on target. With a bear that means the eyes.'

'The eyes?'

'Yes. You have to shoot them in the eyes.'

'What? You mean, not between the eyes,' said Cameron, 'but actually *in* the eyes?'

'Yes.'

'Whoa.' Cameron turned, steadied himself and fixed the screw sight on the bright aluminium ring of the can base, which he had positioned towards him.

'Ok, bear,' he shouted. 'Make my day!' And then he pulled the trigger.

There was a loud 'whoomph' and then a whooshing sound as the bullet streaked harmlessly into the grass.

'Missed,' said his mother.

'Grandmother?' Inuluk had been so engrossed with the boy and the gun that it was only now, as the sound of the shot died away, that she turned towards her grandmother. There was a springing of white fur about Atka's wrists, and a denser ring about her neck. 'Are you all right?'

The reply Atka made was more like a grumble, a growl.

Inuluk looked at her grandmother's face. Her eyes.

There was something very dark there.

'If he doesn't listen,' said Inuluk suddenly. 'If I can't make him understand the stories . . .' She trailed off. 'You wouldn't hurt him, Grandmother. Would you?'

26

Cameron was still awake. He thought he was going to be awake all night. Partly it was to do with the adrenalin still coursing through him because of the gun. How was he supposed to sleep after that? Four direct hits! OK, twenty bullets, so sixteen misses. But four total bull's-eyes!

'You ready yet?' Pascale called. He was supposed to be undressing.

'Not quite,' he replied.

But it wasn't just the gun, he thought. It was also the light. His mother had closed the curtains in the bedroom but they weren't quite generous enough to cover the window and cracks of light remained around the edges. Cameron stepped around the camp bed, meaning to pull the curtain aside to check just how un-dark it was, but the tug on the curtain, the feel of the rough material beneath his fingers and the rattle of the curtain rings, spiked an unexpected memory. He was five years old and he'd been getting ready for bed in the house they'd had when the family was whole, when they'd all lived together. His mother had been away on one of her research trips (possibly even staying on this very island) and he must have been missing her because his father had urged him to come to his bedroom window. Together they'd pulled back the curtains. It was summer, the window was open. He remembered the smell of the night air.

'Blow her a kiss, Cameron. Go on. It'll find her. Kisses can go all round the world, you know. Oh – look, here comes her kiss to you!' And his father, his smooth-talking but often rather stilted, emotionally distant father, had cupped his hands and 'caught' the imaginary kiss. 'Just for you, Cam,' he'd said, as he'd opened his hands against Cameron cheek. 'Feels like a feather, doesn't it, Cam? Mummy's kiss.' And it had. It really had. This imaginary kiss from his mother.

How had he forgotten that?

Cameron found his hand was on his cheek. He was searching for that kiss. And there it was, all of a sudden, feathering up against him and, with it, something more extraordinary still. A wash of love. His *father's*. A love that had snuggled up beside him to read bedtime stories about bears. A love that had opened a window and brought his mother back with that imaginary kiss. Made him feel safe. It was a shock.

Cameron shook himself. Or maybe it was his body that shook, that shivered. He pulled the curtain wide, looked out and beyond, into the midnight daylight.

This window did not look over the inland bay – with its calm water and protective spit – but out over the rougher, outer edge of the island. The Arctic water foamed as it hit the shore. And the sky seemed wider – and lower – than any sky Cameron had ever seen. But then maybe he had never really looked at the sky before. Never looked up.

Had he never looked up?

And just when he was wondering about the sky, the light dazed him. It was extraordinary, it was weird, even eerier than he had first thought.

He looked again, tried to describe it more exactly to himself. It was not full light, more like early twilight, a wash of inky blue with some floating threads of gold. Soft. Strange. *Unearthly* was the word that came into his mind. As though he had inadvertently stepped onto a different planet. The light was also – *diffused*. Wasn't that what his science teacher, Mr Scott, called gases when they spread out a bit, like oxygen did when you went up a mountain? Well, the light was a bit like that too, thin and scattered. But also beautiful and full of . . . well what? Possibilities. Yes, the light seemed full of possibilities.

'Cameron?' Pascale called again.

'Huh?'

'Ready or not,' his mother said, 'I'm coming in five.'

Cameron dropped the curtain, returned to the camp bed and put on his pyjamas. Putting on your pyjamas in daylight. That was pretty odd too. He reached for his Flipcam, flicked it open. Could he broadcast to the nation in his pyjamas? For the sake of etiquette he pulled on a sweater.

'Cameron O'Connor reporting in again,' he began. 'Star Date – 29th July. Star Time – midnight. Or maybe midday. Who's to know? Now, Tom, what would you say,' he continued, returning to the window, 'to a place that never gets dark?' He unlatched the window and shoved the camera out into the air. 'I mean is that weird or is that weird? And it's not just the quality of the light – think about it a minute, a place where the sun doesn't actually set. That means, Tom, it can't actually rise. *The sun rises in the east and sets in the west.* That what Mr Scott told us in Year 7, right Tom? Well not here, Tom. Here . . .'

He broke off, stared out.

'Here . . . it's a parallel universe, Tom.'

He switched the machine off. He was talking rubbish. He couldn't load that to YouTube. On the other hand, plenty of people loaded rubbish to YouTube. He flipped the machine on again. A thought had occurred to him.

'Dawn,' he said. 'What about that, Tom? If the sun doesn't rise, then there is no dawn – right? And if there's no dawn, then there can't ever be *a new dawn.* As in a new beginning. Because that's what it means. *A new dawn.* A chance to start again, begin again. What sort of world would it be if you could never begin again, Tom?'

What if he could never begin again?

With his father.

His mother.

Did that mean he wanted to begin again? Thought things could actually be different?

His mother who had actually said 'yes' tonight. His mother who'd let him use the gun?

Could he love this island mother?

Could she love him?

And his father. Had his father really become someone else, someone different, since the divorce? Or was it him, Cameron, building barriers, expecting the worst, always on the defensive? And, if only he could reach out – open out – he could find again the man whose love had unlatched that childhood window?

He paused, confused. Was it the light making him think this way, letting him see things in a different way? *In a different light*. That's what people said, didn't they? *I saw it in a different light*. Or perhaps he was just a little more tired than he'd thought. It was, after all, very late. Apparently.

He drew the camera in, shone it at his face.

'That's all for now, folks,' he said. And then he added, 'Night, Tom.'

But it wasn't night.

It was day.

27

Dr Pascale O'Connor – up, dressed and breakfasted by 7.15 a.m. – was not in a good mood. She'd specifically requested Dougie as her Park Ranger for the week because he was reliable. At least more reliable than some of the others she'd been allocated over the years. She looked at her watch for the umpteenth time.

'I said eight,' she said to Cameron who was (to her surprise) also up, dressed and breakfasted.

'It's only ten past,' said Cameron.

'Fifteen past,' said Pascale.

'Didn't you say the Inuvialuit had a different understanding of time to us anyway?' offered Cameron.

'Not that different,' said Pascale, grimly. 'If he doesn't come soon,' she added, beginning to pace, 'you'll have to help me.'

'Me?' said Cameron.

'Yes, you. Data-logging, well that's a one-person operation. But slump measuring, you need two for that.'

Cameron thought quickly. He hadn't jumped up in order to measure some random ice-thawing mud! He'd jumped up because, well – he'd pretty much promised to meet Inuluk, hadn't he? Not that he could mention this fact, Inuluk being a girl and his mother being – imaginative.

'Thing is,' said Cameron, 'I've got these lists. Flora,

fauna. Birds! Guillemots. Golden Plovers. Loons. All sorts of loons . . . Remember?'

'You can check them off as we walk,' said Pascale.

'But I couldn't film,' said Cameron quickly. 'I mean, you have to wait with birds. Be really patient, set up a good shot . . .'

His mother stared at him.

'I'd just slow you down,' Cameron said.

'Not as much as not having an assistant will slow me down,' said Pascale.

'I'm sure Dougie will be here any minute,' said Cameron, grabbing for his windcheater. 'And I did promise Dad, you know . . . Do a video diary. For him.' Cameron paused. 'And Christine . . .'

And maybe it was the mention of Christine that set Pascale's mouth into a thin, hard line. 'Well, you'd better have this, then,' she said and she thrust something at him.

'What is it?'

'A map, Cameron.'

'What about the gun?' he asked.

'What about it?'

'Don't I need the gun? I mean to keep me safe and everything?'

'I think you'll be a lot safer with this,' said Pascale, and she clipped a can of bear spray to his belt.

28

Inuluk and her grandmother were sitting together on the ground where the north end of the spit joined the main part of the island. The sacred ground. They might have been sitting there all night, or all day, or for ever.

Inuluk was rehearsing the First Lesson. *In the beginning was Raven,* she muttered. *Raven beat the world into being with his wings . . .*

Atka was silent. She was thinking how it was to these lower slopes that the *Qallunaat* woman always came first. How she brought her instruments and measured things without ever knowing – or asking – what this place actually was. How she trampled here. But then, Atka thought with a sudden pang, how could anyone know what she knew about this land? Unless they too had been dressed at birth by their mother in underclothes of bird feathers, with a cap of Arctic hare fur, and a hood made from the skin of caribou fawn with the ears attached?

Inuluk broke off from her recitation. 'How soon before they're here?' she asked.

'Soon enough,' said Atka.

But it wasn't both *Qallunaat,* just the boy, who suddenly marched over the blind ridge, coming straight at them. Atka stood up, but Inuluk was not so fast. Perhaps she was mesmerised by the boy's approach and the fact that his eyes, instead of watching his feet on the difficult terrain, were fixed on the huge, flimsy sheet of paper he held in front of his face. Her legs were not outstretched, but he managed to blunder over them anyway. Somehow caught the toe of his trainer under the arch of her ankle and tripped just as you might do on the root of a tree.

'Oh,' cried Inuluk.

And Atka caught herself thinking: *This is how the Qallunaat are in the world. Blind and blundering.*

'Oh my gosh, wow, sorry,' Cameron said, as his trip took him three or four paces further forward before he could right himself. 'I just didn't see you there.'

Inuluk nursed her ankle.

'Are you OK?' He thought he might have twisted his own ankle but he wasn't going to mention that. So he just hopped a little.

'I'm fine,' said Inuluk. 'What about you?'

'Fine, totally fine.' He stopped hopping. 'Really. Gosh,' he repeated idiotically. 'I mean anyone would think I was finding this crucially interesting.' Cameron shook the flimsy paper, glad to have something to do with his hands. Glad to have something to cover his confusion. And extremely glad to make it seem like a total coincidence that he'd happened upon her again.

'What is it?' asked Inuluk, from her place on the ground.

'A map,' said Cameron.

Her face was all puzzlement.

'You know – a *map*?' he emphasised.

'Can I see?' asked Inuluk.

'Sure, though being Herschel there isn't that much to see.' Cameron knelt and spread the map out on the ground beside her. 'Just the general shape of the island, a few contours, the cove . . .'

He was pointing at things. The drawing was strange, Inuluk thought, it made the island into the shape of a polar bear's head, with the lake for an eye. Certain places were marked with crosses or rings. Not any of the important places though.

Atka was looking too, over their shoulders. She was thinking of the winter her father taught her to find her way by observing the furrows ploughed in the snow by the wind. 'An Inuit,' Tuligaak would say, 'can never get lost in his own land.' What use would this map be in the snow?

'But what's it for?' asked Inuluk. 'This – map?'

'To find your way about, of course,' said Cameron.

'But surely,' Inuluk said, astonished, 'if you follow such a map, you only find what you know to be there already?'

'Yes,' said Cameron. 'That's sort of the point.'

Inuluk remained amazed. As if one could know everything! As if the land – with all its mysteries – could be captured on a piece of paper!

'Some cartographer – that's a map-maker, by the way – does all the work for you in advance,' continued

Cameron. 'And bingo, there it is. All nice and neat and written down.'

The white man writes down everything, Atka offered as if it was an explanation. *What is not written down, does not exist for him.*

'But,' Inuluk couldn't help asking, 'what about the other things?

'What other things?' said Cameron.

The things that weren't written down. Could never be written down. The things that were whispered and shared in memory and dream and story and song. The secret places. The sacred places. The knowledge of the ancestors. The things that gave shape and meaning to life. Inuluk opened her mouth, but Cameron was speaking.

'I mean they're pretty good, these map-making people,' said Cameron. 'Can take pictures from space, you know. Like who'd have thought there would be a church and a graveyard on this island, for instance?' he added, tapping a strange symbol on the paper. 'Though church is a bit of a stretch apparently – Mum says it's really just a shack with a bunch of nesting guillemots.'

Not guillemots, Inuluk. Her grandmother's mind-thought was sudden.

'Not guillemots?' Inuluk replied aloud. For her mind was not on guillemots but on mysteries.

'Not guillemots? What not guillemots?' said Cameron.

No – ravens! This is your opportunity, Inuluk.

'Oh,' said Inuluk. 'Ravens.'

'Ravens?' said Cameron. What on earth was she on about?

'Yes. In the church,' said Inuluk. 'They aren't guillemots, they're ravens.'

'I'm sure I read guillemots somewhere,' said Cameron. 'Well, same difference, I guess. Birds anyway.'

'Not the same at all,' said Inuluk, catching her grandmother's eye. 'Ravens, ravens are . . . sacred.'

Yes!

29

'Ravens? Sacred?' said Cameron. 'You're joking.'

Inuluk's eyes lit. 'Raven beat the world into being with his wings.' She said.

At last! Lesson One. And so it begins, Inuluk!

'Right,' said Cameron. He paused. 'Can't say we ever covered Raven in comparative religion.'

'Raven made earth and soil,' Inuluk continued, 'planted his world with lichen and grasses and pea-pods.' She was moving as she spoke, or rather she was leaping, flying. The ground was particularly hummocky here and she was flying from grassy knoll to grassy knoll, light and quick as a bird. 'Over every single plant, Raven waved his wings so it would grow and flourish.' Inuluk waved her wings, or her arms anyway.

She was feathery swift and (Cameron thought suddenly) quite enchanting. 'After five days,' Inuluk continued, 'one of the pea-pods burst open. Inside' – she was quite close to him now– 'was a fully formed . . . MAN!'

'Oi!' Cameron exclaimed, the *man* being very loud and right in his ear.

'Raven,' went on Inuluk, who appeared more beak and claw now, 'flew down to earth to inspect his new creation. *Who are you?* He said. *And what are you doing in MY world?*'

'Ridiculous!' cried Cameron and pulled away from her. 'I mean what sort of god doesn't know everything? That's the whole point of a god.'

Inuluk dropped to her haunches, her face a mask.

'Gods,' he continued, 'are all-seeing. All-singing. All-dancing. That's what makes them gods in the first place.'

She was crouching in the same Arctic yoga position she'd been in when he first met her. He seemed to be standing over her, berating her. But he couldn't quite stop himself. 'Besides,' he added, 'you can't have a god who makes people by accident. I mean where would that leave you and me? I mean we'd just be mistakes. Cameron O'Connor, God's big blunder.'

'Yes,' said Atka, aloud.

RAVEN

30

Less than half a mile away, Dr Pascale O'Connor was still in the cabin.

She checked her watch. Thirty-five minutes late. She checked it again.

Forty minutes.

Deep breath.

Maybe Dougie had misunderstood the meeting place. Maybe instead of 'cabin' he'd heard Pauline Cove? Or Collinson Head, or Bell Bluff? Or maybe he'd just remembered that she always liked to start by mapping the hillocks just north of the cabin, where the spit ended and the island proper began? Maybe he had gone to meet her there?

Well, she wasn't doing anything useful staying put and stamping her feet. Pascale loaded up her tripod, levelling rod and magnetic balance telescope and set out. Worst-case scenario, she might be able to catch up with Cameron.

She was nearing the end of the beach when her eye was caught by a flash of white, somewhere near the hill. She immediately grabbed for the small pair of binoculars she always wore round her neck.

'Wonderful!' she exclaimed, writing *Bubo scandiacus* in her waterproof notebook. It was the first snowy owl she'd seen on the island for years. What was it the islanders called them? *Ukpik* – that was it. Harbingers of death, they were supposed to be. If they landed on the hill. She scanned the sky again. Well, the bird was certainly heading that way.

Lucky, she thought, as she put away the glasses, I'm not the superstitious type.

31

On the lower slopes of the hill, Cameron was still talking. Shifting from foot to foot as he spoke, Inuluk noticed how he was trampling on the fluffy white heads of *palliksak*, the island's cottongrass.

'I mean if you don't want to believe in Big Bang theory, fair enough,' Cameron was saying. 'Although I personally rather like the idea of the universe exploding into being out of pretty much nothing.' He paused. It occurred to him to share with Inuluk his view that Big Bang theory was also the only possible explanation for him ending up as Pascale's son. Because obviously only a huge random event or a monumental accident could account for that. But Inuluk seemed to be on screensaver so he just ploughed on: 'But if you have to believe in a god, at least believe in one that actually planned you, wanted you. Like the Adam and Eve bloke. When He made the animals He was only practising. Saved the best for last. His premiere creation – man. Perfect form.' Cameron allowed himself a little twirl. 'Biggest brain.' In case she didn't get the point, he tapped his skull.

Brain of plankton, thought Inuluk. Brain of krill! What was it about this white, southern boy she'd ever found interesting?

Over the ridge behind Cameron came the sound of clanking metal, swiftly followed by the shape of a windcheatered human being.

'Oh,' said Cameron. 'Hello, Mum.'

'Cameron,' said his mother, 'you don't seem to have got very far.'

Correct! Atka's thought exploded in Inuluk's head.

'But I'm glad you stopped here,' Pascale added, plonking down her tripod among the drifts of *Eriophorum*, the white cottongrass. 'You must have known this is the first place I always come to for slump measuring.'

'Mum –'

'Still no sign of Dougie, of course. Unless you've seen him?' she interrupted.

'No,' said Cameron. 'Mum, you haven't met . . .' He looked round for Inuluk. She'd gone very small, was crouching back on her haunches, Arctic yoga style, looking again like the tundra hummock he'd first mistaken her for.

'Bit of a first for the wretched idiot not to turn up at all,' continued Pascale.

'Inuluk,' concluded Cameron.

'No, not Inuluk, *Dougie*,' said Pascale. 'Hold this, can you?' She thrust a five-foot measuring rod at him. 'There.' She flapped him away. 'You need to stand on that hillock, right there.'

Hillock! The *Qallunaat* was pointing at a small mound of sacred earth. *Hillock!*

Cameron took the rod and went where he was directed.

'Mum,' he tried again, and then he saw how Inuluk had sunk right down inside her animal skin jerkin.

Maybe she'd gone all shy, maybe she didn't want to be seen?

Hillock! The repeated mind-thought was maddened. *You will need to move to Lesson Two, Inuluk. Respect for the Ancestors.*

'Put the stadia rod on the peg, Cameron,' called Pascale from behind her tripod.

'Peg?' said Cameron.

'Yes, peg. The metal mark in the ground right in front of you. For goodness sake, Cameron, you don't think I measure the movement of random hillocks, do you? This is science, it needs to be precise.'

Cameron found the mark and watched his mother fine-tuning some telescopic instrument twenty feet away. She had gone into serious work mode. When she was working – and she was almost always working – she had a habit of becoming completely absorbed in the immediate task. As though nothing else in the world existed. It had been like this for as long as he could remember. He gave an embarrassed nod in Inuluk's direction, but he didn't think she saw him.

'Right,' said Pascale. 'Right.' And then: 'You can't tip the rod like that, Cameron. You see the spirit level?'

Inuluk lifted her head a little at the mention of spirit, but Cameron had his eyes on the stadia rod.

'The thing halfway up the rod with the little bubble in it?' said Pascale.

'Yes, OK, I see it,' said Cameron.

'Well, the bubble has to be exactly in the middle

of the two lines for the rod to be level. That's why it's called a levelling rod.'

'Stadia rod. I thought you said it was a stadia rod?'

'A stadia rod *is* a levelling rod, Cameron. Now hold it still. Still!'

He gritted his teeth, held it still.

Pascale fiddled with some knobs. 'Sorry, Cameron, but if it isn't absolutely still and absolutely level, I can't get a reading.'

More gritted teeth.

More fiddling.

'How's the filming going, then?' Pascale said finally.

'Paralysed by choice,' said Cameron. 'The stress of so many fine Herschel locations to choose from, the church with the sacred ravens . . .'

'Guillemots, Cameron. They're black guillemots. The only colony in the western Arctic, in fact. They are on your list. Right, gotcha.' She stood up, compared the new reading from the magnetic balance telescope with the measurements on the printout hung round her neck. 'Thought so. It's definitely . . .'

Shifting.

'Shifting.'

Who needs an instrument to see that?

'Quite significant displacement, I'd say. Since last year.' Pascale started folding up the tripod. 'We might be out with our global warming estimates. It might be happening more quickly than we thought.'

'Dr O'Connor.' A man in western clothing but with

an Inuit face had appeared soundlessly over the horizon that led from the cabin.

'Dougie,' said Pascale. 'You're here at last, then.' She paused, possibly expecting an apology, and when one didn't come she added: 'Done this one already, thanks to Cameron. Cameron – meet Dougie. Dougie – Cameron.'

'Pleased to meet you,' said Cameron.

The Inuit nodded.

'Right, no time to lose,' said Pascale, and she loaded Dougie with the tripod, the levelling rod, the magnetic balance telescope and her computer and marched him away.

32

Cameron watched his mother going, how she strode off up the hill, leaving the Inuit to follow a few paces behind, lighter on his feet than her, despite the gear.

'Bye, Mum,' he called to her back.

If Dr O'Connor heard, she did not reply.

Cameron turned to Inuluk who was standing now, her face clearly visible.

'Sorry about that,' he said. 'She doesn't mean to be rude.'

'I just don't think she – saw me,' said Inuluk.

'Yeah, well, welcome to my world,' said Cameron.

'And . . . Cameron?' Inuluk halted.

'Yes?'

'I . . . I'm sorry about the ravens. I think they might be guillemots after all.'

'Oh great,' said Cameron. 'One more point to Mother. Mrs Always Totally Right.'

Lesson Two, Inuluk, Atka's mind-thought nudged.

'*Respect for all the ancestors,*' Inuluk replied automatically, as if in answer to a prayer.

Cameron looked at her. 'What?'

'I could show you the burial ground,' said Inuluk. 'If you'd like?'

No . . .

'Terrific,' said Cameron. 'Might just dig myself a place there.'

The teaching, Inuluk. I never said the ground, itself. Just the teaching!

But Cameron was already shaking open the map. 'OK. That'll be north. North-north-west to be precise. Right?' He refolded the paper. 'What are we waiting for?' And he set off with a powerful stride, not unlike his mother's.

'Not that graveyard,' said Inuluk from behind him.

Inuluk!

Cameron spun about. 'What do you mean – *not that graveyard*?' He tapped his paper. 'There's only the one marked on the map.'

'That graveyard is for your people. My people, my ancestors we are buried . . .'

Be silent!

'But grandmother, if he sees with his own eyes, he will understand!' Inuluk spilled out.

'What?' said Cameron. 'See what with his own eyes?'

I forbid it, Inuluk.

'And who's the "he" anyway?' Cameron continued. 'Who's Grandmother for that matter?'

Inuluk sighed. 'My grandmother,' she said.

'Your grandmother?' said Cameron. 'You talk to your grandmother? Like – you know – she's right here?'

'Of course,' said Inuluk. 'Because she is here.' Inuluk couldn't help gesturing at Atka as she said this.

Cameron followed the line of Inuluk's arm. His friend was waving at thin air.

'Oh – OK. Let me guess – it's all this graveyard talk. It's brought the ghost of your gran –' he put on a spooky voice, did an elaborate 'brrr' noise with his lips – '*from the Beyond!*'

'The ancestors don't come from beyond,' said Inuluk simply. 'They are here in our world.'

There was a wide-eyed seriousness to her face, a kind of shining innocence. Truthfulness even. Cameron stared at her. She looked a bit other-worldly herself. In fact, he thought, she looked a bit like an angel.

'They stand beside you,' Inuluk continued. 'Journey with you in dreams. Bring knowledge from the past. Speak their wisdoms.'

'Or try to,' said Atka, aloud.

And that's when Inuluk turned, shifted her gaze from the absent grandmother and caught Cameron's eye. Caught him looking. Staring.

'Tell you what,' said Cameron quickly, to cover his embarrassment. 'Why don't we get on down to the graveyard and see how many more fun ancestors we can dig up?'

33

Kick myself, thought Cameron. *I could kick myself!* But actually he just kicked the nearest grassy hummock. He was walking. Where to? Who cared! Over the hill and far away, for all it mattered.

How many more fun ancestors can we dig up?

Shouldn't have said it.

End of.

He hadn't meant it disrespectfully, of course. It was a joke. To cover the staring. Anyone could see that. Anyone but Inuluk, that is. What was it his mother always said? Humour doesn't always travel. Fair enough. But for things to go so very wrong? A perfectly reasonable conversation (well, reasonable if you minused the talking-to-grandma bit) ending in sulks and silence? That was the problem with girls. So temperamental! One minute she'd been all serious and shiny and gung-ho to show him the burial ground and the next – zam! It was like someone had taped her angelic mouth shut. No it wasn't on the map and no she wasn't going to show him after all. And then everything had become just a little weird, not to mention awkward and . . . and he'd had to walk away.

Walk away! From the only interesting thing on the island.

Her.

He kicked another tussock.

Plugged in his iPod.

Unplugged his iPod.

The music didn't interest him. Or rather he couldn't hear the music. Not any more. It was being drowned out by his thoughts.

About her.

Which was ridiculous because he'd only just met her and in any case she was extremely foreign. Foreign. Weird and extreme. They had nothing in common at all. And if they hadn't been thrown together on an Arctic island with nothing else to –

'Oh, Mum!'

Dr Pascale O'Connor had stopped with her equipment again. Had her tripod set up with her magnetic balancing telescope. Only this time it was Dougie who was standing on a hummock twenty yards from her, holding the stadia rod.

'Mum, where's the burial ground?'

'What?' Pascale was looking through the viewfinder.

'The burial ground. Where is it?'

'And hello again to you,' said Pascale, finally looking up. 'Hope you're having a nice afternoon.'

Well, if she was going to be like that! He turned away.

'You could try looking on your map,' she said to his back.

Cameron wheeled about, took the map out of his pocket, opened it up and ripped it in half.

'Not that burial ground,' he said.

'Oh.' Pascale closed the shutter on her machine. 'Let's start again, shall we?'

Cameron looked at her face. 'Sorry,' he said. And then more slowly, 'I'm . . . sorry.'

'OK. Good.' Pascale ignored the torn map. She chose instead to gesture to the Inuit. Stand him down, Cameron supposed. Stand him at ease. The Inuit never moved. Stayed in exactly the same position, holding the stadia rod, as if he was a statue. What was it with these local people and stillness?

'So,' Pascale continued, finally giving him her full attention. 'What happened? What's the matter?'

'Nothing,' said Cameron.

Pascale waited.

'Only well, I was just wondering . . . Because that graveyard on the map. It's by a church. So it's obviously a Christian place, so I was just wondering, you know, about the island people. Where they buried their dead? That's all.'

'Oh. Smart thinking,' said Pascale. 'Well, of course, the missionaries did manage to convert some of the island people so some of them are buried there. But mainly, the locals buried their dead straight into the ice.'

'The ice?'

'Yes. The permafrost. Didn't bother with coffins much either.'

'So – what, they just dug them in anywhere?'

'No, not anywhere. There were – are – certain sacred grounds. In fact the main site is fairly near where we were this morning. Though – if you're thinking of filming, there's not much to see.'

'Where we were this morning?' Cameron repeated. 'You mean – where you were slump measuring? I didn't see any gravestones.'

'Not much to see, as I said. And no stone on the island, for the record,' said Pascale. 'It's just all soil. Remember?'

'And that soil,' said Cameron slowly, 'is shifting . . .'

'Yes,' said Pascale. 'Which is why the locals can get pretty touchy about the sites.'

'Get touchy?' One local was certainly very touchy! 'Why?'

'Why do you think?

Cameron thought. There was an answer – but it wasn't a very nice answer. In fact it was quite a scary answer.

But also an exciting one.

'Right,' said Pascale. 'Have to get on.'

So she began getting on and Cameron began walking straight back the way he'd come.

34

But which way was straight back? If only, Cameron thought, he hadn't ripped the map! On the other hand, there really had been very few things marked on that map so maybe he'd be better off using his eyes? Trying to remember? He just wished he'd paid a bit more attention as he walked. Looked about him a bit.

He looked now.

Noted where the hill was (behind him) and where the sea was (to his right – at least the spit bit was) so obviously he needed to walk that way, keeping the spit bit of sea to his right, because then he'd have to arrive eventually where the spit joined the mainland. He was just congratulating himself on his command of the island's geography (and thinking maybe Inuluk was right, maybe on a tiny island like this a map was a waste of space) when something caught his eye.

It was white and flying.

He squinted upwards. A huge bird, with a powerfully wide wingspan. It occurred to him to get out his Flipcam. But he didn't. He just – looked. He'd never seen, he thought, such a beautiful snow-white bird. It was gliding, idling, floating on the air currents. Was it an owl, he wondered? Surely owls only came out at night? But then, of course, there wasn't any night here. He stared after it. It seemed bigger than an owl should be and also more playful. It was making its swooping, almost joyful way – where? Behind him somewhere. In the general direction of the hill. He followed it until it went beyond a ridge and dropped out of sight.

Fancy stopping to look at a bird! Lucky Mum wasn't here to see, Cameron thought as he turned for the burial ground again.

He watched where he trod – even though he knew he was still some way off. Had to be careful where he put his feet in case the scary (exciting) thing was true. But, for the moment, the land about him was green. Hummocky, grassy green. And also not green. There were flowers. How could he have missed them? There were – oceans of them! White fluffy ones which, he realised, might be the cottongrass his mother always talked about. The stuff the caribou ate. And yellow ones too, with large petals, like poppies. And great spires of blue-purple flowers.

He was coming closer.

There were hillocks ahead but also mud.

A sudden brown gash in the landscape.

The locals can get pretty touchy about the sites.

About the ice. About the melting ice around the bodies of the dead.

But – even looking at the mud – it didn't seem very likely. It still seemed the stuff of stories.

For surely the ice hadn't melted that much? Surely the hillocks hadn't slipped and shifted enough – for instance – to open a grave?

35

Inuluk and her grandmother sat on the grassy edge of the burial ground. They had not moved since the boy left. They'd watched him go – striding away with his temper – but they had said nothing to each other. Not then, not since. Their silence was not aggressive, not blaming. Perhaps they were practising *quinuituq*. And perhaps it was this deep patience that kept their thoughts quiet.

So Inuluk did not say: *I never meant to show him the burial ground, Grandmother. It just came to me that maybe Cameron's mind does not work as our minds do? Maybe he needs to see things – touch and feel them for himself, in order to know, to understand? Maybe stories, maybe being told, for him, is not enough? For I think he may really be a different sort of being, Grandmother.*

And Atka did not say: *In all your life, child, you have not challenged me before. This is a mark of your respect. Challenge is a hard thing for an elder to accept. But be assured, I'm pleased for you and with you. For it shows your own progress. And there will come a time – though not for a while yet, I hope – when your challenge will become a matter of life and death. For a young bear must always challenge an old bear. That is the way of nature.*

No. The two of them did not speak. Even when Cameron clumped back over the horizon. For there was a peace that came with sitting in the sacred ground close to the ancestors. And a stillness that lent their bodies the same shape and form as grassy hillocks around them.

36

Cameron had arrived. At least, he thought he had arrived. It was difficult to tell. The slopes and hillocks managed to look simultaneously familiar and unfamiliar. As though they were just the same as they had been an hour or so ago, but also subtly different. As if they'd moved a little . . .

Don't start! He instructed himself. Just look. *Look!*

He was searching for the slightly lopsided shape of the hillock he'd stood on that morning with his mother's stadia rod. That hillock would be safe. That mound could not be a grave. Dougie was a local. He would never have let Cameron's mother conduct her experiments on a grave. Would he? If Cameron could find the little round metal marker – his mother's 'peg' – then he'd be sure. Use that hillock as a vantage point to look for – what he was really looking for. He strode over to what he thought was the relevant mound and was about to drop to his knees and search the grass for the 'peg' when he checked himself.

What if it was a grave after all?

Ridiculous. There was grass on it for one thing!

But then graves often had grass growing on them. Why did he keep saying 'grave'? Who said it was a grave? No one. That's who.

But what if it was?

What if they all were?

He looked about him. So many tufts and hillocks. What if, beneath each waving green grass hump was a corpse just waiting to burst through?

His felt a thud in his ribcage. It was his heart. His heart was banging in his chest. But how could his heart be banging in his chest when all he was doing was stepping around some grassy hillocks? Melting graves, opening graves, things from the beyond – they were midnight stories. Yells and screams from the dark. And he was just doing a little bit of investigation. A bit of science, checking out a little bit of global warming of his own. In the *daylight*. For heaven's sake.

What was *that*?

It moved. He was sure it moved. A crease of mud beyond the grassy tufts to his left. The mud moved!

'Graves ought to be marked!' Cameron shouted.

'So many dead and so few to bury them.'

It was Inuluk's voice. Cameron spun around.

'Inuluk?'

But she wasn't there.

'Inuluk?'

Unless she was one of the hillocks, one of the tufts of ground he'd first mistaken her for.

Get a grip! You're imagining things – in broad daylight. *What's wrong with you?*

'There – there!' It moved again. He was sure. This wasn't a small crease of mud. This was a hollow, a dip, sunken earth. As though the soil was falling in, being sucked down.

'Inuluk!'

No Inuluk. Obviously no Inuluk. Luckily. He'd hate her to see him stumbling about like this. And he was stumbling now, as though the ground was actually moving, although it couldn't be. Because soil doesn't move like that, certainly not at the speed this soil was moving. Except in films, when there's an earthquake and a road just splits in two and cars disappear down the crack and . . . and . . . and not sunken now, but widening, more mud, more earth, the grass being pulled apart, forced apart and the soil, heaving, gulping.

And something in that earth.

Something white and thin and bony hard, and him falling (falling so hard and so fast it almost felt like he was being pushed), falling full length into the erupting earth with his hand instinctively outstretched as though to break his fall. But that hand actually going down, down through the yielding soil towards the thin, hard bony thing.

'No. NO!' He was trying to pull his hand back. But he couldn't. There was something on his hand.

It was Atka. Or rather Atka's staff. She had the gnarled end of it on Cameron's wrist. She was pressing down, as if she and the spruce were one together, the weight of a tree.

For the boy was not welcome here. That had been made quite clear. So if he chose to come, if he chose to put his hand where no hand should go then why shouldn't he feel the horror that was his own doing?

And Cameron wanted to cry out again – would have cried out but his face was in the dirt. And the dirt in his mouth.

'Grandmother!' Another shout. And this time it was Inuluk. Her feet anyway, at ground level, where his eyes were. Where had she come from? Where exactly had she come from? Out of the shifting soil?

No – not soil shifting now but air. The air above him seemed to flurry and move and the weight that was pressing on his hand seemed suddenly released and his face sprang from the earth and also his fist. In his hand was a long, curved –

'Bone!' screamed Cameron. 'It's a bone!'

'Grandmother!' admonished Inuluk.

'Grandmother,' yelled Cameron, leaping to his feet, mud sputtering from his mouth. 'It's your grandmother's!' And he flung the bone as hard and far as he could. 'That's way gross.' And then he spat. And spat.

'No,' said Inuluk.

'That's disgusting!' Cameron was wiping his mouth, his tongue. He was also almost crying.

'No – wait.' Inuluk crossed to where the bone had landed, picked the bleached thing up. 'It's animal bone,' she said. 'It's caribou.'

'Caribou?' said Cameron, his heart still jumping, 'Caribou!'

'Yes,' said Inuluk. 'So be still, Cameron.'

37

Be still! All right for her to say! 'But this is the burial ground,' Cameron said. 'Isn't it?'

'Yes,' said Inuluk. 'But where you' – she paused – 'fell, that was not a grave. And this is not a human bone.'

Of course not, thought Inuluk. Atka would never have guided Cameron – pushed him indeed (for Atka had pushed him) – into the opening earth where her ancestors were buried. It was not, after all, as if Atka needed a headstone to remember where the graves of her forebears were. Inuluk nevertheless felt justified in giving her grandmother a hard stare.

'Look,' she added to Cameron, holding out the bone for him to see.

It was a thin eighteen-inch curve of bleached white.

'Caribou?' Cameron repeated.

'Yes,' said Inuluk.

Of course, caribou. The mind-thought was mild, as if some of the fire had gone from Atka. As if, seeing Cameron scream and yell, was, for the time being at least, triumph enough.

'You're sure?' said Cameron. He needed to be sure. He needed things to be normal. He brushed earth from his trousers. His hair. He controlled his voice. He looked back where he'd fallen. It was just a patch of earth. Slumping earth. But only earth. Not really opening much at all. How could he have fallen there?

'Yes,' said Inuluk.

'How can you be sure?'

'I've skinned caribou. Eaten them.' Inuluk paused. 'It's a rib bone.'

'Right,' said Cameron. 'I knew that.' He finally reached out and took the bone from her, ran a finger the length of the curve. 'Or would have done, if you could order a bargain bucket of Kentucky Fried Caribou.' Another joke. *Another idiotic joke!* What was he thinking? 'I mean,' he added quickly, 'it's way too big to be a human bone, right? I mean, imagine God pulling that from Adam's chest!'

Inuluk said nothing but her eyes discomforted him. He had a sudden, irresistible urge to apologise. But what for?

For shouting and screaming and being an idiot?

For being curious about the sacred ground? Well – it was her who'd first mentioned it!

For the erupting graves themselves? How was that his fault? He could hardly be held accountable for global warming. After all – he was only a boy! Only one insignificant boy in a whole world of – well, other people. And anyway, it was a touchy subject. Probably best not to go that place.

So?

So he needed to move on. Get back to a place of conversational safety. Try to find that space they'd been in in the morning. Put all the embarrassment and the falling over and the being covered in dirt behind him.

'Inuluk . . .' he began.

'Yes?' Her eyes were still dark.

Apologise. *Apologise!*

'Inuluk – I'm sorry . . .'

Was that a smile coming?

'. . . about your pea-pod story,' he finished.

'My pea-pod story?'

'Yes. I'm sorry I laughed at it. That was like Mum, wasn't it? Just plain rude.'

And then Inuluk laughed. It was a silvery sound.

'Doesn't matter,' she said.

Doesn't matter? Of course it matters! Atka's mind thoughts were sharp again.

But Inuluk did not react to her grandmother's anger. 'Would you like to hear the end of the story, then?' she said shyly.

So. The coming of Polar Bear. Good, Inuluk. We will teach him of greed and of fear!

'You mean there's more?' said Cameron.

'Yes.'

'Perfect. Totally perfect. Where's the Story Corner?' *He'd done it!* Somehow he'd done it! Arrived back in that happy place. Stories. He'd remember that. Stories were her happy place. He felt strangely relaxed. Almost light-headed.

'Story corner?' she repeated.

'No – sorry. Forget it.' *Don't blow it now, Cameron.*

'I'll just settle down here on the nice warm grass. So long as that's OK with you, I mean,' he added quickly. 'So long as this isn't – you know – a grave or anything?' Because, all of a sudden stumbling into a grave didn't seem quite so appealing any more. In fact, it seemed almost disrespectful. 'You know it would sure help if you people marked your graves,' he couldn't help adding. 'I mean fair enough no stone, but you could mark them with wood. Have you seen all that wood down at the beach?'

Inuluk's face suggested she had seen it.

'So many dead and so few to bury them.'

'What did you say?'

'I said – sit here,' Inuluk said.

So he did. Sat on a small (presumably safe) mound of springy lichen and kept quiet. Because perhaps he didn't want to hear what he thought he'd heard her say, that ghostly echo: *so many dead and so few to bury them*. Perhaps he wanted to get away from death and the dead, retreat into the comfort of story time. Or perhaps he just wanted Inuluk to be a bird again.

For there she was.

Flitting around him, her eyes beady-bright and her voice lilting, musical. She was just as she had been in the morning, when she'd flown hummock to hummock telling him the first part of the story. Don't fly away, he thought. Never fly away.

'Raven asked man if he was hungry,' Inuluk said. 'And when man said he was, Raven flew away to find heath berries. Man swallowed the berries in one gulp.'

Her head pecked forward and he heard the gulp in her throat.

'Raven knew then that the berries would not be enough to feed his new creation. So he set about making seals and walrus, filled the rivers with fish, set birds in the sky. Every creature that Raven made, Man looked at with pleasure. Raven was afraid that Man would eat up the whole earth.' Inuluk paused. 'So he made polar bear.'

Cameron was in a daydream, he was transported. 'Sweet,' he said.

Sweet? Atka's mind-thought thundered. *Sweet!*

'Raven,' explained Inuluk, 'made polar bear so man would have something to fear.'

'Fear?' said Cameron.

38

'Raven made polar bear to stop man's greed,' added Inuluk, spelling it out for Cameron.

Never, thought Atka, *did I ever have to explain the meaning of this story to a Inuvialuit child.* She watched Inuluk's words float away, breeze over tundra.

Cameron shook himself to his feet. 'Have you ever seen a polar bear, Inuluk?' he said. 'I mean – up close?'

'No,' said Inuluk, quickly, stealing a look at her grandmother. She had a sudden premonition that this talk of polar bears would not end in a good place.

'I saw one once,' Cameron said.

'You?' Inuluk's voice was all surprise. 'You saw a bear?'

'Yes.'

Atka was swiftly behind him. 'And did you feel the fear?' she breathed.

Cameron swatted at his face, as if at a mosquito.

'What sort of bear?' asked Inuluk

'A green one,' said Cameron.

'Green?'

'Yes, green. Well, bluish-green to be exact. Their fur is hollow, according to Mum. It had sucked up a load of chemicals and algae from its swimming pool.'

'I don't understand,' said Inuluk.

'The bear,' said Cameron, 'it was in a zoo.'

Fur spiked at the back of Atka's neck, her nails pricked where her claws were bedded. And, from somewhere in a belly deeper than hers, came the beginning of a growl.

'*Pisugtoq?*' said Inuluk, stunned. 'Caged!'

'*Pisugtoq?*' said Cameron.

'The Ever-Wandering One. That's what we call him. Because he wanders alone over all of the ice.'

'Well, that day,' said Cameron, 'he was wandering behind a nice high fence.'

The growl was rumbling, gathering throat and power.

'Well, not fence exactly,' continued Cameron. 'A moat, around the enclosure, and then a high glass wall. So you could see him pad about. Or her pad about. One of them was definitely female.'

'Pad about?'

Atka was out on the ice: she was cresting Mount Newton in Svalbard, she was making her way to Nanortalik, two thousand miles to the south-west. She was walking, wandering searching for food. When there was no food, she would walk quickly, up to a hundred miles a day. Where the sea ice was thin, where a human couldn't walk, she would skate like a water strider, her belly sprawled low to the frozen ocean. The sea, the land, her territory. She walked it, smelt it, knew it all.

'Quite a big enclosure,' said Cameron. 'Thirty metres across or so. And they do have a pool, as I said. A pond thing, to dive in. You know, when it's hot.'

Atka was diving, her body flowing to the sea floor in search of mussels and kelp. She was idling twenty miles from shore observing a shoal of fish. She was waiting patiently by an *aglu*, an ice hole, for the emergence of a seal. She was standing on the sea ice, her platform for hunting. This ambusher, this flesh-eater. She was preparing to dive again. And again.

'They growl a bit,' Cameron said. 'And they pad. Or this bear padded. And there was a moment when I thought she looked really bored. If a bear can look bored. But they do give them toys.'

'Toys?' said Inuluk.

'Yes, big plastic balls. And the bears push them about.'

Atka opened her jaws and a sound came out of her mouth that even Inuluk had never heard before. A wild roar, a roar of pain and anguish. It was so loud and desolate and savage that Inuluk thought the whole world would hear it.

But Cameron heard nothing.

39

'Cameron,' asked Inuluk, standing up and coming close to Cameron, so she could look into his eyes, 'what sort of fear do you have in your world?'

'I don't know. Same sort you have probably.'

How can you? Atka was shaking. Not so much with anger now but with exhaustion. She was tired of it all. Tired in her soul. 'How can you,' she repeated, aloud, 'if there are fences? If there are moats and walls of glass between you and the thing of terror?'

'If you're safe,' said Inuluk, 'how do you feel the fear?'

'What?' said Cameron.

His eyes seemed empty.

The words. There was weariness in Atka's mind-thought. *Tell him the words, child.*

'*Kappia,*' said Inuluk. 'The fear of danger. When maybe the ice is too thin to take your weight.' It made her shudder, not the word itself, but the image that came with it, the sheets of thin, flexible ice. Ice floating on a dark sea. She felt the sudden chill of that sea and heard her friends calling, as if it had been yesterday. The voice of Oyangin and then, more frantic, Putagor: *Jump, Inuluk. Jump!*

'That sounds well cool,' said Cameron.

Well cool!

'*Irksi,*' continued Inuluk. 'Terror.' She turned away

KAPPA
The Fear of Danger...

so as not to see her grandmother's face as she added: 'When the ice storm comes and there are only thirty seconds to find shelter before you freeze to death.'

'Mega-cool,' said Cameron.

If Atka was thinking now, she kept those thoughts to herself.

'And *ilira*,' finished Inuluk. She was talking to Cameron but listening for her grandmother. She heard only silence. Had her grandmother gone already? Gone to her own place of terror?

'*Ilira*?' Cameron said.

'The fear that accompanies awe,' said Inuluk. She had to finish the lesson.

'Don't get it,' said Cameron.

'The fear you have,' said Inuluk, 'when you stand before a polar bear. Or an unkind father. People or animals who have power over you and you cannot control or predict.'

'Unkind fathers?' said Cameron suddenly. 'Why is it always the fathers? What about unkind mothers?'

'And white people,' said Inuluk.

'White people?' said Cameron. 'Why would you fear white people?'

'Because of the killing,' said Inuluk. And then, because Atka was still silent, Inuluk added: 'So Grandmother says.'

40

'Inuluk says we killed her people,' Cameron said later that evening. He had been pacing the very small space between his camp bed and his mother's, whacking the caribou bone rhythmically into the palm of his left hand as if it was a small whip. But now he poked his head into the ante-room.

Pascale was busy at her computer, entering data and looking at graphs. She'd been busy all evening, barely spoken to him. Except to say 'no', of course.

No, sorry Cameron, I'm too busy for shooting practice tonight.

And:

No, you can't have a go by yourself.

'Inuluk says there were two thousand of her people on the island before the white man came,' Cameron added when she didn't reply. 'And by the time we'd left only two hundred. That's a ninety per cent death rate.'

He was standing foursquare in the doorway now.

Whack, went the caribou bone. Whack, whack, whack.

'Mm,' said Pascale.

'That's the equivalent of the Inuvialuit coming to England today and wiping out' – Cameron did some quick mental maths – 'forty-five million of us!'

'Mm,' repeated Pascale.

'Is that all you can say– *Mm*?'

'I'm working,' said Pascale.

Whack, whack, WHACK.

'There was this little girl apparently, five years old. She woke one morning to find the whole of her family had been wiped out. Not just her mum and dad but all her extended family, her aunts and uncles, her grandparents. The whole community – gone. So she set off walking, no food, nothing. She walked and walked. The whole way from the island, over the frozen sea to the mainland. Got one hundred yards away from a settlement, one hundred yards from safety – and then she just collapsed. Collapsed in the snow. She never got up again.'

Pascale raised her eyes from the screen. 'Haven't heard that one before. Locals normally tell you about how men used to keel over playing poker.'

'You don't care at all, do you?' said Cameron.

'Well, it was a very long time ago,' said Pascale, 'and it's not as if we killed them deliberately. '

'Really? Not what Inuluk says.'

'Look, no one got a gun and lined them up and shot them one by one. They just got white-man diseases. Tuberculosis, measles, flu.'

'Flu? Since when did flu kill anyone?'

'More often than you think. When you haven't met a disease before, you just don't have resistance. And it didn't help that the Inuvialuit thought the solution to a high temperature was to take off their clothes and roll around in the snow. Now' – Pascale looked at her watch – 'it's getting late, Cameron. Why don't you get ready for bed?'

41

Inuluk sat in the night-time sun. It was summer, it was warm, but not in her mind. She was standing on the dancing ice. Sea ice is not like fresh-water ice. Fresh-water ice is fragile and clear, and it breaks like glass. It does not deceive you, not like *tuglu,* the shore ice that forms in October under the moon of *Tugluvik.* Salt-water ice is opaque, flexible, slightly elastic. Sea ice follows the swell of the ocean without breaking, it draws you, calls you. *I am safe,* it whispers, *come.* All Inuvialuit know this about the deceitful *tuglu* and yet they come still, the young ones. They come to the shore to play on the floes. To jump.

To test their nerves.

Had she sought out Oyangin that last ever day? Or had Oyangin come with her twin brother Putugor and said: It's time, again. We're going to the shore, Inuluk.

The adults saw them leave and no one called them back. When there is ice, everyone must take responsibility for himself. There was no goodbye.

'Grandmother . . .' Grandmother had her terror and Inuluk had hers. That was just the way it was.

'Yes, child?'

'Being near Cameron,' Inuluk said, 'it's made me think about my friends again. Oyangin, Putugor.'

'Turn your mind away from that,' said Atka sharply.

AVUNNIVIK

THE FEBRUARY MOON When the Seals pup

TUGLUVIK

THE OCTOBER MOON When the Sea Ice forms

ITARTORYUK

THE NOVEMBER MOON When the freezing Mists come

NUERTOVIK

THE JUNE MOON When the harpoons are hurled

'I can't,' said Inuluk. 'I hear their voices, I hear them calling just as they used to, just as they did that last ever time.'

'Enough,' said Atka.

'And then I'm back out on the *tuglu*, and all at once Putagor's shouting louder and louder – *jump, Inuluk, jump!* But his voice is going dim and the darkness, the sparkling darkness, it's beginning to close over my –'

'Enough, I said,' Atka thundered. 'Do you want to break your heart – and mine – all over again?' She took a breath. 'The task is what's important now. Let us just concentrate on the task, Inuluk.'

42

Cameron had put on his pyjamas but he was not in bed. The constant daylight meant that his body seemed uninterested in sleep. He had paced all the floor there was to pace in this small room so now he was standing at the window, trying to get a little air. As he looked across to the outer edge of the island, where the Arctic ocean pounded the shore, his thoughts returned to the five-year-old child who had once walked over that water to the mainland – and the wolf pack that had followed her tracks back to the island.

Yes, that's what Inuluk had said. Wolves had never been seen on the island before, but this pack – a pack larger than any ever known in the Yukon – had followed the stench of death northwards. The family of the five-year-old – dead of the white man's diseases – had not been buried. There had been, as Inuluk pointed out, no one left alive to do the digging. So the wolves came to feast. But, though there were many dead, there were not enough to feed the ravening pack, so the wolves took to devouring each other. It sounded like a story, it sounded as if it could not be true. Wolves operating in too large a pack, wolves crossing a frozen ocean to a killing ground too far away to smell, wolves turning vicious fangs on each other. But there was something in the way Inuluk had told the story – as though she had seen these things with her own eyes (though she readily admitted it all happened long before she was born) that made it seem true. He wanted to ask his mother about it, but he didn't want her just to brush him off again, as if the answer didn't matter.

Thwack went the caribou bone in his hand.

There was one question, however, to which he did need an answer. A question which continued to nag at him. He dropped the curtain at the window and, in fewer than five paces, was at the door of the cabin ante-room.

'Mum,' he said, 'why did white people – why did we – come to the island?'

Pascale was still tap, tap, tapping on her keyboard.

'I mean in the first place? Why did we come?'

Pascale didn't even nod his way, just went on tapping.

'I mean before global warming raised its totally fascinating head, that is.' Cameron added.

Tap. Tap.

Tap. Tap.

Tap, tap, tap.

'Are you getting totally fascinating scientific results?' Cameron yelled.

Tap, tap, tap.

'Mother!'

'Now you know what it feels like to me when you're on your computer all the time,' said Pascale.

43

Inuluk and Atka were sitting together on one of the grey tree trunks. Inuluk was rubbing her thumb back and forth over a knot in the wood that even the sea hadn't managed to make smooth.

'I'm not doing the task well, am I, Grandmother? Nothing I say reaches Cameron. His mind – I think it's on other things.'

'Mind!' exclaimed Atka. 'Oh yes, that great mind his god gave him. A brain that believes no other animal exists. That he is entitled to eat up the entire planet!' Atka stood up and Inuluk was alarmed at the set of her face. 'I have decided,' she declared. 'It is time for a different sort of lesson.'

'No!' said Inuluk.

'Yes. A lesson he will never forget. An encounter with a real bear. I see no other way.'

'No, Grandmother. Please!'

Atka turned away. 'I do not think the *Qallunaat* understand stories any more,' she said. 'The boy must learn in his bones what terror is.'

'Lesson Three – the dreams,' cried Inuluk frantically. 'We haven't tried the dreams!'

'I do not think the boy's soul is big enough for the dreams,' said Atka.

Inuluk came to stand foursquare before her grandmother.

'I do,' she said and her eyes blazed.

Atka paused then, looked at her granddaughter. 'You are a good child, Inuluk,' she said at last. 'Your patience is deep indeed.' And Inuluk would need all of that patience when she came to understand the real task that was set for her. A millennium of patience during which – enduring which – Inuluk would have to hold on to everything that was of importance. No matter who or what stood in her way. And all she would have to fight with would be her own hope and goodness. 'Yes,' continued Atka. 'You will make an excellent Guardian for the island when I am gone.'

'Guardian?' said Inuluk.

'Yes,' repeated Atka quietly. 'Surely you knew?'

44

'The people, Mum.' Cameron was not going to be deflected. He was standing in the ante-room now, less than a crate's width away from her. The crate that had started off as a dining table and which, somehow, had become her desk. Her All Important Desk. If she didn't answer he would kick that crate. 'Why did the white people come here in the first place?'

Pascale sighed and clicked 'Save'. '*Balaena mysticetus,*' she said.

'*Wingardium leviosa!*' Cameron countered, twirling the caribou bone like a wand a little too near to her face.

'Latin anyway. And don't do that, Cameron,' she said, pushing the bone away.

'Latin for what?'

'The bowhead whale,' said Pascale. 'People came here to kill whales.'

Cameron put the bone down. 'Why would anyone want to kill a whale?'

'Baleen.'

'Baleen?'

'Think plastic before plastic was invented. Baleen's stiff but highly flexible – and a bowhead's mouth might contain 700 plates of the stuff. Whales use it for filtering krill from water, like a giant sieve. And the Victorians – well, they had many uses for it: buggy whips, parasol spurs, fishing rods, shoe horns, tongue scrapers, you name it. But its premiere use was probably for the whale-bone corset. Thousands of whales harpooned so the ladies of London could look thin.'

Pascale delivered this litany without emotion: it was a list, it was information, it was history. But that was not how Atka heard it through the open window.

'Wait here,' Atka had said to Inuluk, only moments before. 'If the boy is to travel in dreams, I must know what is on that great mind of his tonight.' And she'd set off for the cabin.

Now she stood – and trembled – at Pascale's words. She was no longer an old woman standing outside a dilapidated cabin, she was a young girl with her first sight of the white men's boats and the blood in the water. She heard the thrang of the harpoon's flight, how it hit between the whale's shoulderblades, the tip exploding three seconds later, to splinter and lacerate its way into the whale's flesh. She saw again how the whale – who had no enemies in the ocean and therefore no thought of attack – thrashed as her lungs collapsed and she was heaved towards the boat on a thick, tarred rope. The rope was attached to springs in the boat's hold, strong springs, designed to twist and turn and defeat her.

'Then there was the oil of course,' Pascale went on. 'Before petroleum. Whale oil and blubber. It was used for candle wax, street lighting, soap, margarine, lipstick, detergent . . .'

Atka remembered how, to bring the creature aboard,

they pierced her blow hole or sometimes her lip, the edge of her smile, to fit a tow line. How huge metal tongs clawed her up the slope to the flensing deck where men wearing spiked boots (to keep their balance on her back) would slice her flesh with long-handled knives, ten foot strips at a time. And still the whale would smile. Though distorted now as parts of her body were thrown below into the mincing digesters.

It was enough for Atka. She didn't stay to hear Cameron say: 'So she was right.'

'Who was?' asked Pascale.

'Inuluk,' said Cameron. 'Killed her people. Killed the whales. Killing the island.'

45

'Killing,' said Atka to Inuluk, who had waited by the tree trunk. 'They talk of the whales their people killed. And the possessions they made from the killings.'

'That's good,' said Inuluk.

'Good!' exclaimed Atka. 'Imagine a whale singing of the buttons she'd carved from human bones!'

'No,' said Inuluk, 'good because we can dream Planet Sea. Take Cameron underwater. Of all the journeys you ever took me on, Grandmother, I always loved Planet Sea the best. Do you remember? What you used always to say to me?' Inuluk's eyes sparkled. '*If whale had named the world he would have called it not Planet Earth but Planet Sea. So little earth. So much sea.*'

The memory soothed Atka. She took her granddaughter's hand. 'You remember well, child.'

'If we take him there, Grandmother, he'll see for himself. Lesson Three. Dreams and Understanding. How no creature on earth depends on us for their life. But we depend on them. How we are visitors here but the animals – they belong.'

The child gave her strength. 'Let us go, then,' said Atka.

Together they returned to the cabin. As they passed the open window they heard Pascale say: 'The Inuit killed whales too, you know.'

'But we didn't just cut their mouths and leave their headless bodies floating on the ocean!' cried Atka.

'Grandmother,' said Inuluk. 'Grandmother . . .'

But Atka was not to be stilled. 'We only killed to eat. Took nothing more than we needed to live. And each time we took, we gave thanks to the animals.' Atka was back with her father, Tuligaak, as he knelt on the black beach of Qikiqtaruk before the leviathan body of an Inuit kill. She watched him pour clean, fresh water into the whale's mouth, keeping silence and bowing his head as he did so. 'The death of an animal is a gift,' he had told Atka. 'An animal chooses his own death, chooses the hunter to whom he will submit. There is a bond and a respect between hunter and hunted. If we lose this bond, Atka, if we do not respect those who give up their lives, then our lives will be lost too.'

'This is your final warning, Cameron,' said Pascale. 'Bed!'

'But I won't sleep,' said Cameron.

'Yes, you will,' said Pascale.

'Yes, you will,' whispered Inuluk.

'Yes,' said Atka. 'You will.'

46

If (like the ancestors) you had watched Inuluk and Atka gain entry to the cabin that night, you would have been surprised how effortless it was, how they seemed to flow like wind, from outside to inside. So if Pascale had been aware of anything (which she wasn't) it would only have been the sensation of a slight breeze, or the flap of a curtain, or the creak of a wooden door. But then there was always a slight breeze and a flap of a curtain and a wooden door creaking in the cabin at this time of night. It was nothing unusual.

Besides, Pascale was working.

So she never saw the two figures who passed through the ante-room and came to stand by Cameron's bed.

Cameron was lying on his back, bathed in the soft light of the night. His eyes were shut tight. He had said he would never sleep, but there he was: deeply, solidly asleep. Fast in his dreams.

Atka had known that this is how it would be.

'Will you journey with him?' she asked. 'Or shall I?'

'I will, Grandmother.'

'Then let us begin.'

Atka breathed slowly, evenly, let her mind loosen. Then she held her hands high over the boy's chest and spread her fingers wide.

'Feel your skin,' she whispered, 'your whale skin.

It's slightly furrowed to the touch, your velvet black colour softened by grey. Your eyes are brown and dark. Three times the size of caribou eyes, but tiny in your huge head.'

And the way Cameron moved beneath those hands, rocked a little, might have made you think he heard those words.

Inuluk began to pace, marking a circle about Cameron and letting Atka's words feed into her memory. She remembered the first time her grandmother had taken her to join the white whales at Nalroreak, where the Mackenzie River flows into the Arctic Ocean, she remembered the dark water of Baffin Bay and the sounds of the seals at Imariuk. At first she kept each sea journey separate in her mind, a circle for each, then she gradually let the edges of her rememberings dissolve, until she no longer knew where one journey (or one circle) ended and another began: where the real flowed into the imaginary. She dreamed, as her grandmother had taught her (and her grandmother before that), with her eyes open.

From somewhere beyond and above her, she heard Atka's voice: 'Are you ready, Inuluk?'

Inuluk stopped circling.

'Yes, Grandmother.'

'You have lips and a smile,' said Atka, holding her spread hands above Inuluk as well as Cameron now, 'but you don't have gills. You cannot breathe underwater.'

Cameron shifted then, turned over, gave a little moan.

'You have a blow hole,' continued Atka. 'A blow hole so sensitive to the touch that if, when you sleep at the surface of the ocean and a bird chances to alight softly upon you, you start wildly.'

As she said this Inuluk reached out and touched Cameron on the top of the head.

He jolted, jumped up, stood swaying on the bed. 'What?' he shouted. But his eyes were glazed. He was still asleep.

'Good,' said Atka, 'good.' She waited for the boy to gain his balance, watched the way his body moved in the air. When she was sure he was composed she said: 'You're going to dive now. Take the breath. Take it now!'

Cameron opened his mouth, he sucked in a huge lungful of air.

'Go with him, Inuluk,' said Atka urgently.

Inuluk also took a large lungful of air, felt how it flowed into her blood, how it pumped her heart deeper and faster than usual.

'Now take his hands,' instructed her grandmother.

Inuluk stepped quickly up onto the bed, her weight shifting Cameron's balance.

'Careful!' cried Atka.

Inuluk reorganised her feet, reached for Cameron's hands, touched just the tips of his fingers.

'His whole hand,' said Atka. 'It's his first time. Do not let him go, Inuluk.'

The in-breath was in Inuluk's muscles now. She grabbed for Cameron's hands, held them tight.

'Now dive,' said Atka. 'And remember, his breath will last no longer than *arviq*'s.'

Fifteen minutes, thought Inuluk. The breathtime of the bowhead whale.

'Now dive. Dive!'

The water came then, not the wetness of it but the pressure. It bore them both down, down. The pressure of a mountain, of ten mountains, pushing them down into the dark. Eyes useless, blinded. Nothing to see but the dark. But as their eyes dimmed their bones hollowed. They became air cavities, the spaces in their skulls, their teeth, their breathing passages all became ears, as though their travelling bodies were acoustic instruments, perfectly tuned to hear the music of the deep.

Just like the bodies of whales.

47

Cameron was floating, flowing, flying. Dreaming. It was one of those dreams when you're not quite sure whether you're actually awake and dreaming of being asleep, or asleep and dreaming of being awake.

He did know he was in the dark, but he was not afraid. In fact he had never before felt so comfortable in his surroundings, so sensitive and so alert to everything around him. If anyone, anywhere in the world, were to tip just one extra teaspoon of water into the ocean, he thought, I would know it, feel it.

Just as he knew (how could he know?) that the bubbles that were bursting against his skin were caused by a shoal of cod cruising unseen a hundred yards ahead of him. The bubbles flurried, a thousand small kisses against his flank. He experienced each one individually – their tiny pops and explosions. Heard them, not with his ears but with his whole body as if he was a drum and the bubbles minuscule drumsticks.

It took him another moment to realise that he wasn't just vibrating with the movement of the cod. He was fluttering – quivering – with a thousand different ocean sounds. The reverberations (which seemed to be trembling his heart as well as his body) could have been overwhelming, but Cameron found he could listen separately, let single sounds wash around and through him, as though the score of this watery sym-

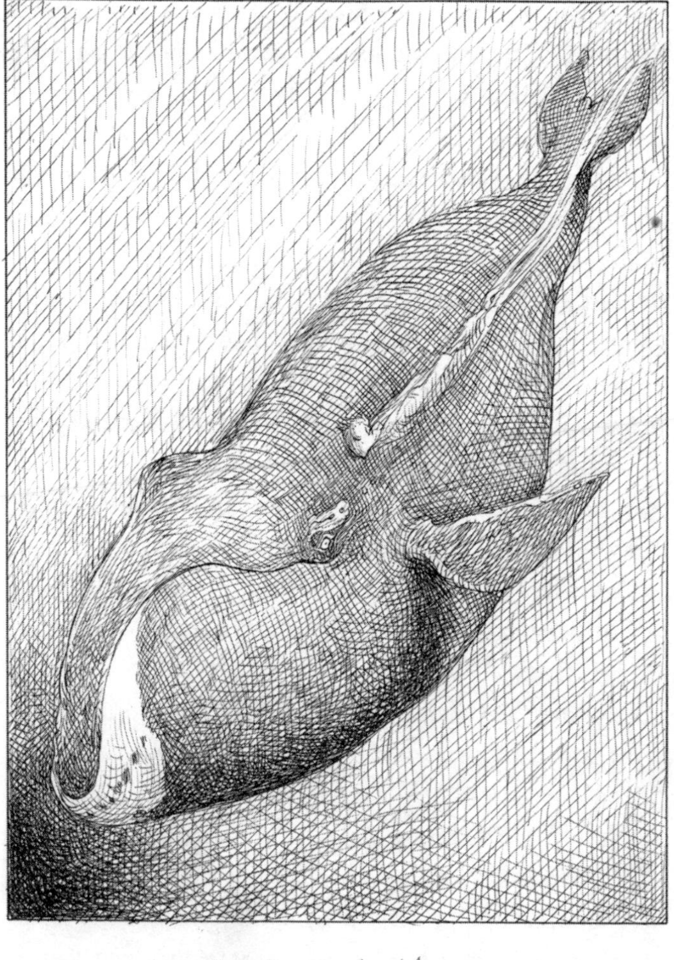

DREAM

phony was somehow familiar to him. He could distinguish the high tunes and the low: the dark, grumbling turbulence of sediment shifting on the ocean floor, the plaintive whine of fracturing sea ice. And, closer by, the call of individual sea creatures. The long, wild tremolo moan of –

'*Urgruk*.'

The voice was Inuluk's. Inuluk was here with him!

'We call him *urgruk*,' she repeated, 'the bearded seal.'

And some part of Cameron wanted to reply, 'I know. Of course! *Urgruk!*' For he had that strange sensation you have when you return from abroad and the incomprehensible babble of foreigners suddenly becomes the perfectly understandable language of your own people. But how could he recognise the language of the bearded seal?

'And that booming,' said Inuluk, 'it's *aiviq*.'

Cameron felt the baritone noise echoing in the hollow of his ribs.

'Walrus,' he cried. 'It's a walrus, isn't it? And that . . .' He paused to concentrate on the dog-like yelps and barks.

'*Natchiq*,' said Inuluk.

'Ringed seals!' said Cameron. He wasn't even sure he could picture a ringed seal, though his mother must have shown him photographs. But it wasn't that sort of knowing. It was a knowing like a muscle knows – deep, instinctual.

'And that,' said Cameron, 'that electric crackling, snapping. It's shrimp, isn't it?'

'Yes,' said Inuluk. 'Arctic shrimp, krill, sea-butterflies. A swarm of them, a million strong. Which is lucky because you eat them.'

'I do?' said Cameron.

And there in the water was Inuluk's laugh again. Bubbling, joyous.

Cameron caught himself thinking: 'I want this to last for ever.'

And that was before the singing started.

Every bone and membrane and tooth and hollow of Cameron heard the song. It came from far away, perhaps from halfway around the planet, or perhaps from a tucked-away place deep inside him, a place deeper than memory.

Harmonics, bird-like trills and clicks.

'Narwhal,' said Inuluk, 'with a horn like the unicorn. Mythic creature speaking to its own. '

'Belugas,' said Cameron as he recognised a different, pure calling tone. 'Beluga whales.' He didn't even know he knew the word *beluga*.

Then a sudden trumpeting.

'Arviq,' they cried together. *'Arviq!'* And here was another language he'd never been taught. 'Bowhead whales!'

'A tribe,' said Inuluk. 'A nation. Our nation. Whales who have circled the planet for forty-five million years. All the stories of forty-five million years!'

Reveries of loss and love and wonder. The thrashing of flukes on the surface of the ocean and the secrets of the dives below. Secrets shared across the Atlantic, the Pacific. The submarine song of a new-born calf, the solo-concert of a male in love, the joyous chorus of a whole pod arriving home to their breeding ground.

Cameron opened his mouth (and his mouth seemed huge) and emitted a sound that he had never heard before, never known, never imagined that he could contain. It wasn't a particularly impressive sound. It was more of a pulse, a push, a stutter, a squeak. But it was truthful. It was an attempt to speak.

And from somewhere around the planet, a reply came. He thought it was just an echo but then he realised that the pulse of his own song (for, despite everything, that's what it was, his stutter, the first few notes of a song) was not just being repeated, it was being re-invented. Halfway round the globe, a whale was improvising, responding, singing back.

Greetings, sang the whale. *Welcome.*

48

Inuluk was gliding. A millennium might have passed or maybe just a few minutes. *Joy can do that,* she thought, as *arviq*'s breath circled her heart. *Joy can free you. Make you let go.* She hadn't let go of Cameron though (she would never do that) but he was so confident, so natural in the water now, that she took a moment to call up to her grandmother: 'You see? You see!'

Which is when it started.

It didn't begin gradually, it didn't start small and build, it came suddenly, ferociously.

'No,' cried Inuluk. 'What's that?'

It sounded a little like the propeller of a ship, only bigger, more churning, as if a thousand propellers had been lashed together and were suddenly turning in unison, grinding their way into the sea bed.

The noise was so loud, and the vibrations so violent that the ocean and all the creatures it contained seemed to churn with it. They turned and squirmed, they dived and plunged. But they could not block their ears, for their whole bodies were ears.

'No,' cried Cameron as he spun away from her.

'Cameron!' She was so sure she had been holding him, was holding him. But the noise was disorientating her, making her nauseous, sick. 'Cameron!'

'Get off me,' shrieked Cameron. 'Leave me alone. Get off me!'

But she wasn't touching him.

'Inuluk!' It was her grandmother's voice, cutting through the dark and the churning. 'Come up for air. Come now!'

Inuluk was spinning. Spinning. She felt a huge whoosh of water and then something spun harder and faster past her.

It was Cameron.

'Now!' shouted Atka. 'Surface, Inuluk. Breathe.'

'Ow, ow ow!' screamed Cameron. And his *ows* seemed to turn in time with the machine. For that's what it was, Inuluk realised as she was sucked towards it – a huge, drilling machine.

'Leave him,' said Atka. 'Look to yourself , Inuluk!'

'No,' Inuluk screamed. But it was only one scream among all the screams of the ocean creatures. She was being whirled and thrown, along with the seals and the walrus and the fish; all of them dazed, wretched, calling and not being answered.

Leave him! Atka commanded again.

Inuluk remembered the adults who never said good-bye as she went down to the tuglu shore. *Every Inuvialuit must take responsibility for his or her own decisions.* But this journey had not been Cameron's decision. It had been hers.

'Cameron?' she cried. 'Cameron!'

Only the drill answered. It whirred and sucked and spat and ratcheted. It flung rock at her. In the dark and the roiling, Inuluk thought she could make out one shape bigger than all the rest. She began to swim towards that thrashing, floundering shape.

She would lift him, push him, guide him, carry him on her back if she had to.

She would surface with Cameron – or not at all.

49

The child was impossible, Atka thought. And wilful. Had she learnt nothing? But then, the instruction had been clear: *It is his first time. Do not let him go.*

Atka reached through the water, through the depth of the dream. It was further than she had ever reached before and two was always harder than one. It would sap her strength and bring the end closer, but then the end was close now anyway.

'Inuluk.'

She felt a rush of love, just calling the child's name aloud. *Inuluk*. Inuluk the Impossible. A Guardian needed to be impossible. Impossibly brave, impossibly hopeful. And wilful. Hadn't they always said that of her? *How wilful you are, Atka*.

'Inuluk?'

Success demanded absolute calm. Atka shut out the machine noise. She held aside the displaced moans of *urgruk*, refused *natchiq's* panicked yelps. She listened through and beyond the surging, rushing, water. And located –

The boy.

But she had reached for Inuluk, followed the trace of the heartbeat she knew and loved so well. How could she have mistaken the boy for Inuluk?

'Inuluk? Inuluk!'

No answer.

Atka quelled a rising panic. She pushed the boy aside, pushed past him, reached deeper still.

And there, beneath the *Qallunaat*, weighted down by him, crushed and drowning yet again, she found her granddaughter.

Would things never change?

50

Inuluk felt the pull. Felt herself being hauled through her own imagination, up, up. She didn't have time to be grateful, the breath was almost gone from her body, her muscles were spasming, and she needed all her remaining energy to hold on to Cameron. He was flailing, twisting against her, dragging them back down under again, yet so long as Atka held her, she would hold Cameron.

'Cameron . . .' She could barely speak. 'Please . . .'

Yet still he thrashed.

Crashed.

Cried.

Bawled.

Exploded back into the cabin shrieking: 'Don't do it. No. No! Leave me alone!'

'Cameron?' In the ante-room, Cameron's mother heard her son. 'What is it?' She came into the room, a rectangle of light framing her in the doorway. 'Whatever's the matter?'

Focused as she was on her son, Pascale didn't notice the two figures collapsed in the shadows. But then there wasn't much to notice. The exhausted old woman and her exhausted granddaughter were humped together like a pile of rags.

On the bed, Cameron continued to thrash and moan.

'Cameron!' Pascale came to his side. 'Wake up. Wake up! It's just a dream.' And she shook him by the shoulders.

'Dream!' shouted Cameron. And suddenly he was awake, very awake. He was standing on his bed, rippling with shock and adrenalin. 'Nightmare! I was – a whale. I was a whale! And there was this harpoon, coming right at me and then it wasn't a harpoon but this massive, massive drill thing and it went right in me, pierced me right here!' He pointed at his side, his ribcage. 'And instead of blood, you know what poured out of me? It was oil!'

'Whoa, whoa. Steady on,' said Pascale. 'Calm down. Sit.'

Cameron sat. His head was spinning. He was sure there was something he'd left out of the dream, but he couldn't remember what.

'Deep breath,' said Pascal. 'That's it. Take your time.' She paused. 'All that talk of whale killing, I'm afraid. Not the best pre-bed subject, probably.' And she took his hand and held it. And he actually let her, didn't snatch his hand back, didn't bat her away. She stared down at her son's hand in her own. It looked strange, that link of hands, so long had it been. Time passed slowly. So slowly she came to feel a little embarrassed, disengaged herself. 'Now what would you say to a mug of hot cocoa?'

Cameron didn't say anything but she got up and made him one anyway.

When she returned, he was still sitting in exactly the same position on the bed only his head was in his hands. 'You all right?' she asked.

He looked up and she couldn't quite work out whether he seemed dazed or thoughtful.

'Here,' she handed him the cocoa. He curled his hands around the warm mug.

'You are right about one thing though,' she said, watching him drink.

'Hm?'

'The drilling. We are drilling for oil here.'

'What?' He was suddenly on high alert again. 'And killing whales? We're killing whales again!'

'No, of course not,' said Pascale. She made her voice very calm, very reasonable. 'In fact, a few years ago, I was part of the Canadian think-tank discussing oil exploration here. It was a very thorough piece of work. We considered everything. Even drill noise.'

'Drill noise?' he repeated. Just saying the words made him feel nauseous again.

'Yes. Some of my colleagues were worried that drill noise would interfere with the sea mammals' echo-location systems. But you know what? We reckoned there's so much ambient sound down there anyway, the whales wouldn't hear a thing.' She patted his sleeping bag. 'So you can sleep tight, Cameron.'

51

On the cabin floor, Inuluk shook herself of exhaustion, letting her immediate surroundings come slowly into focus about her.

'Grandmother?' she whispered.

The old woman did not reply. Her eyes were closed and she looked frail and grey. She needs to be out in the open air, Inuluk thought. Qikiqtaruk. I have to get her into Qikiqtaruk's air.

She slid one hand behind her grandmother's neck and the other under her knees. It was only then that she realised they weren't alone in the room. There was a shape moving about Cameron's bed.

Pascale.

Inuluk halted, held herself still in her crouch. But Pascale had her oblivious back to them. She was fiddling with mugs and pillows.

'Grandmother,' Inuluk breathed in the old woman's ear, 'I'm going to carry you.'

The old woman was airy light, just a wisp of something wrapped in animal skins, no heavier than the stick she always carried with her. Yet Inuluk felt herself clench, tense. She couldn't help feeling that she was about to transgress, to lift something way beyond her capabilities.

For hadn't it always been Grandmother who was the strong one? Grandmother who – over all the years –

had carried her, borne her aloft?

'I'm so sorry,' she mouthed as she took the barely breathing old woman in her arms and crept towards the outside world.

52

'Goodnight,' said Pascal at last. 'Goodnight.'

Cameron was asleep almost before the second 'good-night'. Poor boy seemed totally worn out. Probably the change of air. Pascale stood a moment watching the rise and fall of his chest.

The last time he shared a nightmare with me, she thought, he was seven. It was the recurrent one about suitcases. He'd dream that he was standing in the hall of their old house watching a suitcase walk down the stairs all by itself. He was rooted to the spot, unable to run, even though he knew, when the suitcase got to the final step, it would yawn open and eat him up. Normally he woke up just before the suitcase got to the bottom. But on this one night, he'd woken after the case had opened.

'Pink,' he'd screamed. 'Inside it was pink, like a mouth!'

It had taken much more than milk to calm him that night.

Looking at him now, Pascale had a terrible urge to lean down and kiss his sleeping cheek. Sleep always seemed to smooth the roughness from him, soothe away his daytime anger. It reminded her of how he was when he was a tiny baby. How she'd routinely wake in the middle of the night and listen for his breathing. How she'd get up, come and stand, as now, close to his bed, just to make sure he was still alive.

She wouldn't kiss him now, though. Of course she wouldn't. Not even a peck, a touch. What if he woke?

She would just gaze – gaze on her beautiful boy.

How long did she stand there gazing?

She didn't count the time though eventually she found herself back in the ante-room. She switched off her computer, tidied her papers. She folded away a briefing document from the oil company that was part-funding her research. When she was done she opened the door of the cabin and went to stand for a moment in the open air. The midnight daylight was shimmering.

'I love this island,' Pascale heard herself say aloud.

Yes. She loved the rolling tundra, the white cotton-grass and the sparkling sea beyond. Loved the island's spits and slumps, its bluffs and deltas. Loved the way the sun neither rose nor set but simply rolled over like a huge lion on the horizon. Looking at the midnight sun – and thinking of her sleeping boy – Dr Pascale O'Connor allowed herself a rare moment of joy.

NUANNAPOQ
the extravagant pleasure of being alive

53

Atka was aware of her granddaughter's apology. She was aware, as Inuluk carried her through the anteroom of the cabin, of the flickering of a machine on the *Qallunaat*'s desk. She was conscious of the slightly sour smell of coffee dregs and, once outside, she could feel the wind on her face, the sweet island wind which came in from the sea with a slither of ice in it. She was aware of these things but away from them, as if a curtain divided her from the real world.

I must have shut down, she thought, suspended.

She had survived like this before: it was *pisugtoq*'s way, when food was scarce and times harsh, to enter a state of walking hibernation. It allowed one to live, when there was nothing to live on. The effort, the reaching, had drained her but now, as she felt Inuluk lay her down on the soft tundra, as she touched the soil of Qikiqtaruk, smelt its earth, she felt her spirit returning.

'It was my fault,' she heard Inuluk say. 'I should never have suggested the dreams. I'm sorry. I'm so sorry, Grandmother.'

'Your fault?' said Atka, and her voice was deep and surprisingly strong. 'No. Never.'

'No?' said Inuluk who was glad to see her grandmother revive so swiftly. But also alarmed. She knew what would come.

'It was the *Qallunaat*!' said Atka and there was a scratch and growl in her voice.

'The *Qallunaat*?' repeated Inuluk, as if she didn't quite understand, though she understood perfectly.

'Drilling the sea bed and drilling our dreams.'

'But not Cameron,' Inuluk exclaimed quickly. 'You can't include Cameron, can't blame him. It wasn't his hand on the drill.'

'Not today perhaps,' said Atka, who was sitting straight up now. 'But tomorrow? Tomorrow it will be him. I tell you, him and his kind – they are all the same. They never know when to stop.'

'Grandmother –'

'No,' said Atka. 'It is enough.' And she banged her staff into the ground.

Inuluk felt a falling away. She wanted to resist, she wanted to be sure, be sure that her grandmother understood about Cameron. She wanted . . . to sleep. The effort of the dream, the journey, the fear of the drill, the terror of the creatures in the sea around her and the carrying, all that . . . carrying. Supporting Cameron, lifting her grandmother. Carrying . . . carrying them both.

How could she be awake after all that?

Inuluk curled into the earth.

54

Atka looked down at the sleeping child. She seemed so young suddenly, vulnerable.

Atka had a moment of hesitation.

What if her granddaughter wasn't strong enough after all? If she carried out her plan, if she brought the boy to the ice, there would be consequences. An encounter with a bear – it was not always predictable. She must take a moment to reflect, not rush anything, make sure she wasn't simply responding to a millennium of anger. Atka looked beyond the island edge, searching for the horizon, the juncture of sea and sky. She often sought a horizon. A horizon defined a limit and suggested a place beyond that limit. It gave one new perspective. So she looked up, out. Not across the inland bay, but out across the seething ocean.

Her view was blocked, blotted.

Standing between Atka and the ocean was the black shape of a woman.

The *Qallunaat*.

It was the *Qallunaat*!

How dare she stand there? How dare she stand in that place, of all places, looking out over the sea just as Atka was looking? Facing the edge of the sun, the rim of the world, as though everything that lay behind her – the island, the white *palliksaq* flowering hills, the black soil, soil of Qikiqtaruk – was hers?

It was enough indeed.

It was more than enough.

'Fear,' murmured Atka, and she felt the immediate spring of fur on the back of her neck. 'Fear . . .' Her nails were pricking and scratching. 'He shall know fear.' Atka's legs shortened and stoutened, her weight increased and redistributed. She dropped to all fours.

Fear in the bone.

Fear in the blood.

Atka's massive right paw landed in the earth next to Inuluk's head. She observed herself digging each one of her five claws deep into the soil. The print was large, unmistakable. Atka looked at it with satisfaction. She flexed her shoulders, shook the sweep of her golden white fur.

Then she set out for the cabin.

Pascale, still looking out towards the sea, never heard the low chuff-chuffs behind her or the padding feet. Not even when the bear gathered lumbering speed, moving inexorably towards her quarry.

The bear, by contrast, was sensitive to every movement, every sound of and on the island. As she came closer to the cabin, she could even hear the boy breathing.

In and out.

In and out.

Steady breath and then a yawn and a sigh as he turned in his bed.

Atka growled. It was only a soft growl.

'Pisugtoq,' she said as she entered his room. 'Great Wanderer. Ice-bear. Sea-bear.' Her paws hit the floor in time with her names. 'Nanuk. Isbjorn.' The names trembled the planks beneath her feet.

She came to a stop at the head of Cameron's bed.

'Come then, boy,' Atka growled into his ear and this growl was not so soft. If Cameron had been awake, he might have seen how the bear's lips retracted to reveal (not unlike a certain suitcase) a violet pink mouth.

'Come to the ice,' she snarled. 'Come – if you dare.'

55

If Pascale had turned towards the cabin just a moment earlier, she would have witnessed the exit of her sleepwalking son in the company of a large white bear. She would have seen how the bear nudged the sleeping boy, guiding him with her nose. But Pascale had her eyes still fixed on the horizon and she saw nothing. Which was lucky, because she was a rational woman and if she had seen the bear and the boy, she would not have believed it anyway.

In any case her mind was full of Christine. She didn't want to be thinking about her ex-husband's new partner, but sometimes, when she was momentarily happy, she found herself, willy nilly, arriving at his partners. Amy, Jo and now – Christine. It happened on the occasions when she saw something very beautiful and she wanted to share it. When she wanted to say: look at that! Isn't it amazing!

And the person she wanted to be there beside her in that moment was still – and always – Hugh. Cameron's father. The only man she'd ever really loved – despite what had happened. Despite what Hugh had said.

'You don't have any time for me,' he'd said. 'We don't do anything together. We're not even in the same country half the time.'

And yet, even now, whenever she saw something extraordinary – like the sun rolling around the horizon like a huge golden lion – it was always Hugh she longed for. Hugh who came into her mind. Only he never came alone. He came with his women. With Amy. With Jo.

And now – with Christine.

56

Inuluk, in that hinterland somewhere between being asleep and being awake, heard the footfall of Nanuk, the Great White Bear. She was also dimly aware of a second creature, the lighter tread of an animal walking in a vague zigzag as if it didn't entirely know where it was going. Or was being pushed. She woke suddenly with the panicky heart you get when you sense danger. In her direct eye-line were a pair of bare feet.

'Oh . . . Cameron,' she said, sitting up, slightly bewildered. 'What are you doing here?'

Cameron barely looked awake himself. He rubbed his eyes.

'Dreaming,' he said. 'I think, I'm dreaming.'

'Me too,' said Inuluk.

'I mean I was in,' said Cameron. 'In the cabin, in' – he looked down at himself, registered his blue striped pyjamas – 'my bed. And now . . .' He turned slowly and gazed about him. 'I'm out. And . . . you're out. Should you be out?' he continued, perhaps to cover the embarrassment of the pyjamas. 'I mean – this late? Alone?'

'I'm not alone,' said Inuluk. 'Grandmother's here.' She said it simply, instinctively, and then she looked about her.

Where was her grandmother?

'Oh right, I forgot,' said Cameron. 'The ancestors

are always with us, right? Stand about us. Journey with us' – he paused – 'in dreams.'

'Yes,' said Inuluk, finally locating Atka some way behind her. Her grandmother was dropped in a strange position low on the tundra. Her head was down, her shoulders broad, heavy, like those of –

'A bear,' she said aloud.

'A bear?' said Cameron.

'I was dreaming *pisugtoq,*' said Inuluk, slowly beginning to piece the scene together. 'Polar bear.' She paused and then added. 'A she-bear.' This last was directed questioningly, perhaps accusingly at Atka.

What had her grandmother been doing?

The old woman was rising from her haunches. As her head lifted, Inuluk caught sight of her eyes. They were pin-point dark. Wild. Glittering. Inuluk could not hold her gaze. 'Look,' Inuluk said, pointing down at the earth, 'there are the prints.'

'You can't dream something, Inuluk, and have it walk right by you,' said Cameron.

'No?' said Inuluk. 'That's how my people have hunted for a thousand years.' *Hunt*. As soon as she said the word she knew what that glittering look was, knew what Atka had been doing. She had been hunting!

'I think it's this lack of night,' said Cameron. 'I think it's touching your brain the way it's touching mine.' He came over to inspect the footprint, knelt down, spread his hand over the dirt depression as if to check whether it could have been made by a human hand.

Then he looked up at her. 'You didn't just make this yourself, did you?'

'Me?' exclaimed Inuluk.

'Because if this really is a bear track, Inuluk,' Cameron said, touching the place where Atka's claws had been, 'I think we ought to be making some serious tracks of our own.'

'Don't worry,' said Inuluk. 'The bear's moving away from us.' She made a gestures with her hand, as if she was shooing something away.

'How do you know?' asked Cameron.

'The tracks,' said Inuluk. 'They lead that way. Over the hill.'

'Are you sure? How can you be sure?'

'The bear will have been heading for the shore,' Inuluk said definitely. 'Towards *tuglu* – the sea ice. That's where bears hunt from. The ice.'

Atka was now standing fully upright in the caribou skins of an old Inuvialuit woman. She contrived to look innocent. She shrugged. But there might, Inuluk thought, be a glimmer of having been found out.

'I wouldn't mind if it was dark,' said Cameron. 'If it was dark, you could feel scared – not that I am scared, you understand – and that would be OK. But in this endless light, everything's just plain weird.'

'Endless light?' Inuluk couldn't help saying. 'Sometimes it's so dark here, Cameron, you can see nothing at all. Not your own hands. Your own feet.'

'What – you mean, in winter?' said Cameron.

'Yes,' said Inuluk. And when the storms come. The storms bring white darkness.'

'Now that sounds properly Arctic,' said Cameron. 'I'd like to know what that feels like.'

'Would you?' said Atka aloud, and suddenly she was standing right behind him and the glitter was back in her eyes. 'Would you really?'

57

In the ante-room of the cabin, Pascale changed into her night things, folding her day clothes neatly and putting them on the makeshift crate table. She brushed her teeth, using as little water as possible. She pulled a comb through her hair without looking in a mirror. Then, very quietly so as not to wake her son, she moved through into the bedroom part of the cabin.

She was going to get straight into her sleeping bag. She never had any trouble getting to sleep, she just ran through in her mind the jobs for the following day and then went 'out like a light' as Hugh used to say.

But on this night, she couldn't quite resist having one more peek at Cameron. So she walked the few steps beyond her own camp bed to Cameron's.

Cameron wasn't there.

58

As soon as the words were out of her mouth, Inuluk knew she had made a mistake.

'No, Grandmother . . . please. I'm sorry I mentioned the storms.' Talk of the storms always took her grandmother straight back to the place of terror.

'Grandmother?' repeated Cameron. 'She's . . . really close then, tonight?'

'Close enough to put ice in your eyes, your mouth, you hair!' said Atka. *Tell him, Inuluk!*

'No,' said Inuluk desperately. 'It's not one of the lessons.'

Not a lesson? Atka mind-talked. *It was the hardest lesson I ever learnt.*

'Inuluk?' Cameron went to stand abreast of her, stared into the space that Inuluk was staring into, tried to see whatever it was that she saw. There was nothing there.

When I was just a little girl, a thousand moons ago. Tell it!

'No,' said Inuluk. 'It will break your heart. All over again.'

'Inuluk, are you– all right?'

If we forget the language of the ancestors, we forget how to think. If we stop telling our stories, we stop knowing who we are.

And then Inuluk knew that she had lost. Her grandmother was right, as she was always right. There were things which needed to be remembered. Truths which needed to be spoken. Inuluk turned to face Cameron. 'It was the second winter the whalers were here,' she said. 'Their ships frozen in the bay.'

'What?' said Cameron.

'My mother lay in her bed,' Atka whispered. 'Hot with the white man's disease.' She sank towards the earth, as if someone had stolen the breath from her body.

'The sailors were out on the ice,' said Inuluk. 'They were playing ball.'

When she said the word 'ice', Cameron felt a strange shiver down his back.

'Ash from the ships' furnaces marked the baseline.' Atka said from the ground. 'An old sail was the back-stop.'

'There was nowhere flat to play on the island,' said Inuluk. But the ice was flat. The sea ice. It was minus five degrees when the game started.'

'My father went out to watch,' said Atka.

'Grandmother . . .'

No! Tell how the temperature dropped. As if the sun had died.

'Cold to make rocks shatter,' said Inuluk.

'Inuluk?'

'It's coming,' said Inuluk.

'I hear it always,' said Atka.

'What?' said Cameron. 'What's coming?'

Then he began to hear it too.

59

'Cameron?' Pascale shouted. 'Cameron!'

She shouted for him even though it was quite plain (after all the cabin wasn't very big) that Cameron was not in the bedroom and he was not in the ante-room.

Cameron had gone, disappeared.

But how could he have gone? Where could he have gone?

'Cameron!' Pascale yelled. 'Answer me!'

Cameron did not answer.

Throne Room, she thought slightly wildly. He must have gone to the Throne Room. Only he hadn't, because then he would have had to pass her and she would have seen him. Window, perhaps he'd climbed out of the window? Why on earth would he climb out of the window?

Nothing for it.

Pascale grabbed her anorak.

And the gun.

60

'The wind,' said Inuluk. 'The wind like a thousand knives.'

'Actually,' said Cameron, 'it does seem cold all of a sudden. Look – I think I've got goosebumps.' And he had. Where his arms poked out of his pyjamas he was covered in goosebumps. But it wasn't just that, it was that the land around the them, the ordinary green wavy grass land, the black dirt, it all seemed strangely drained of colour suddenly. Pale. White even. And then there was the sound in his ears, a high whipping, whistling sound that seemed to chill him, chill his face, his ears, his nose.

'Rule of thirty. That's what Mum calls it. At minus thirty degrees Celsius with a wind speed of 30 m.p.h., exposed flesh will freeze in thirty seconds. I always wondered what happened to your eyeballs,' he added idiotically. 'Do your eyeballs freeze?'

'He stood there,' said Inuluk, 'my great-grandfather. Stood there in the white.'

No shadows. No horizon.

'Lifting his feet,' said Inuluk, 'and putting them down again. Up and down, as if he was walking, walking to safety.' And she started walking and Cameron, could see her walking. At least, at first he could. But that was before the blizzard came. The flakes swirling dense about him. And so cold, although it was only a story.

IRKSI
terror

'He thought he had feet,' said Inuluk, 'because they were going up and down, but he couldn't see his feet. Couldn't see his hands.'

Cameron looked for his own hands. But they were gone, swallowed up in the white. And Inuluk, she was gone too. She was just a voice, somewhere in front of him.

'He had thirty seconds to find shelter,' said Atka, aloud.

'Thirty seconds,' repeated Cameron. Though he didn't know if he was repeating himself or something or someone else. The storm made echoes. In another time, Atka would have heard this repetition and been astonished by it. By the hope it held. But – in this moment – she was moving to a place beyond hope.

'He didn't know which way to turn,' said Inuluk.

The wind howled, the ice seemed to be in Cameron's bones. 'What happened?' His teeth knocked and rattled in his mouth. 'Did he make it?'

'No,' said Atka aloud again. For yes, sometimes even after all these years, she needed to speak the truth aloud in order to believe it.

'No,' said Inuluk. 'He died and a friend of his with him. And three white men from the boat.'

Cameron wanted to say something, thought he should say something, but the cold seemed to have closed him down. He couldn't speak for the ice in his mouth.

'The storm raged for three days,' said Atka.

'When the wind finally dropped,' said Inuluk, 'they found the bodies far out on the ice.'

'They'd been walking the wrong way,' said Atka. 'They'd been walking towards the sea.'

'When they told Great-grandmamma her husband had died,' said Inuluk, 'her spirit left her body in that moment.'

'I held her hand as she died,' said Atka. 'They said to me: do not hold your mother's hand. If you hold your mother's hand you too will catch the white man's disease. You too will die. But I wanted to die. I was seven years old. I thought it was better to die than to be alone.'

The white was clearing, evaporating, like so much mist on a summer's morning. It was gone so very quickly. Cameron could see his arms again, his legs. He was wasn't cold, not at all, he didn't have goose-bumps. His mouth was not full of ice. The earth was warm. Midnight warm.

He turned to find Inuluk sitting on the ground. She was rocking, rocking as if she was holding something large and precious to her breast.

'They were buried together,' she said. 'My great-grandparents. Near to where you found the caribou bone.'

She turned her face up to his. Her eyes were dry and piercing bright.

Yet somewhere, very close, Cameron thought he could hear the sound of sobbing.

61

Pascale was running. Even though running on the lumpy, tussocky earth was both stupid and hardly possible. If she had remembered the whistle, she would have been blowing it. But she'd left in too much of a hurry. Forgotten the whistle, forgotten the bear spray. But she did have the gun. Yes. The gun was slung over her back, its butt banging into her spine as she ran. Her childhood rifle. Would she really fire it? Of course she would, if Cameron was in danger. Of course! But a bear, why would there be a bear now? Just because it was night? Light night. No reason to suppose a bear was more likely just because Cameron should be sound asleep in bed.

She wasn't being sensible, she wasn't being rational. She was panicking just like that day when Cameron was three and she'd lost him in Debenhams. She'd been looking for a coat, flicking through the rails. And all of a sudden he just wasn't there. If she'd have had a whistle she'd have blown it then too. Only she didn't have a whistle so she ran and shouted and people thought she was mad and she didn't care. Cameron wasn't there. Not in coats, not in dresses, not in underwear. He'd totally disappeared. And how had she found him? She couldn't quite remember, had blocked that bit out. But there he was suddenly, beyond the double doors onto the back stairs were the public weren't supposed to go. Singing. Singing to himself. Smiling. Quite happy.

Stairs. She'd never thought about that before. The back stairs in Debenhams where he got lost and stairs in his pink-mouth suitcase nightmare. Why had she never made the connection before? But then maybe there wasn't a connection, because she'd lost him in Debenhams's that day, but he hadn't lost himself. He was having a fine old time on those back stairs.

'Cameron,' she yelled. 'Oh for god's sake, how could you do this to me!'

For there he was again, quite unharmed standing out on the lower slope of the hill in his pyjamas.

'Do what?' said Cameron.

'Sneak out like that,' she yelled. 'Without, without... taking bear spray!' she finished.

'I was only talking to –'

'I don't care what you were doing,' Pascale screamed. 'Back to the cabin. Back to the cabin RIGHT NOW!'

62

Somehow she'd bundled him back, bundled him along and in. Pushed and shoved and shouted at him. Thrown her own anorak over him in case he was cold.

'Cold?' he'd wanted to say. 'Yes, I've been cold tonight. Seriously cold. Colder than you could ever imagine.'

Imagine. Was that it? Had he been imagining?

'If it was dangerous for me, it must be dangerous for her too,' said Cameron, once they were back in the cabin. He was trying to locate himself.

'Who?' said Pascale. She was very calm now. She had put away her anorak. She had put away the gun. She had very deliberately (and with great effort) refrained from asking him what the heck he thought he was doing out there.

'Inuluk, of course,' said Cameron.

'Inuluk?' said Pascale. 'Was she out there too?'

'Obviously,' said Cameron.

'Then we have to go back,' began Pascale. 'Get her in –'

'No, no,' said Cameron quickly. 'I mean, I think she's with her grandmother, anyway.'

'Oh,' said Pascale. 'OK.' And then, after a pause. 'I didn't see anyone out there with you, Cameron.'

'Yeah. Just like you didn't see Inuluk that day when you were out hillock-measuring.'

'I'm sorry?'

'You know, when you got me to hold that stadia rod thing? Inuluk was there then too.'

'She was?' Pascale looked at him askance, the way she did when she was about to challenge him, when she didn't believe what he was saying. Her mouth almost opened and then she seemed to clamp it shut again, and, right in the middle of the conversation, she went back out into the ante-room.

Cameron heard a key turn in the cabin door lock.

Fine. Let her believe what she liked. Cameron made for his bed, tripped over his rucksack, sent his Flipcam skittering across the floor.

'Put that away,' said Pascale coming back into the room and seeing him fiddling with it.

'I could show you a picture of her,' said Cameron, remembering how he'd filmed Inuluk on the first day as Lesser-Known Arctic Hummock, David Attenborough style.

'Not now, thank you,' said Pascale.

But Cameron was already scrolling back, flipping past the film about the midnight sun. 'Look.' But he'd gone too far, arrived at his birthday greeting to Tom. He pressed the buttons again, searching more slowly, frame by frame.

'I said put it away.'

He came to the juncture, the end of his first film, *I'm going on a bear hunt,* and the beginning of his second, *Cameron O'Connor reporting in again. Star Date*

29th July. Between the two takes was a frame or two of bare tundra. An Arctic hummock. But no Inuluk.

No Inuluk at all.

63

Inuluk and Atka sat on the sacred ground, close enough to talk but not talking.

Atka had seen the bird the moment it landed on the hill. *Ukpik,* the snowy owl with its startlingly white plumage and its extraordinary head which could rotate a full circle so that, without moving its body at all, it could survey the whole of the island in a moment. And yet *ukpik* was not surveying the island. *Ukpik* was looking directly at her, Atka.

So, Atka thought, the time has come.

It was not unexpected and part of her was glad. But, finally facing the bird, she realised she wanted – needed – just a little longer. So she was careful not to alert Inuluk to the hill, or the bird that sat there. She would spend these last few hours in her granddaughter's company in silent gratitude. It would be enough just to be near Inuluk. In the morning – well, there would always be a morning, even if she wasn't there to see it.

Inuluk, meanwhile, had not challenged her grandmother about the night's events. There was nothing that needed to be said. Atka was still determined to take Cameron to the ice. Inuluk was opposed. Their positions were quite clear. It didn't help to go over things. Besides, her grandmother was frail.

Frail?

How could she imagine such a thing after seeing those wild, black eyes?

And yet.

Inuluk stole a glance at the old woman. For she was old, as ancient perhaps as Qikiqtaruk itself. And like the island, Inuluk realised suddenly, there was part of her that was fierce and enduring and part of her that was as soft as Qikiqtaruk's soil, and could – just as easily– be washed away.

So what, Inuluk wondered, had made Atka endure all these years? What had kept her going? The anger, she supposed. If the task was to be accomplished and the anger to die, maybe Atka would die too? Retreat to the final resting place of all the spirits, all the ancestors?

Inuluk put the thought away. There was plenty of time yet.

64

Cameron was not asleep. His body was dog-tired but he seemed to have lost the off-button for his brain. Just as, it appeared, he must have lost the on-button for the Flipcam. Because that was the only explanation, wasn't it? He'd simply pressed the wrong button, or failed to press any button at all. That, or he'd inadvertently wiped the bit of film with Inuluk.

So how come he did have a picture of the hummock itself?

That was the annoying fact that his brain kept getting hooked on. Fine if there had been the bear-hunt film and it had cut straight to the Star Date one. Not fine if there was a picture of a hummock between the two clips but no picture of Inuluk curled on top of that hummock. But then there was no sound either, no marvellous David Attenborough impression, so perhaps he'd just taken a random shot of the ground at the end of the bear-hunt film.

Yes. That must be it.

So can I go to sleep now, please?

Toss. Turn.

Toss. Turn.

'Cameron, are you still awake?'

'Mm.'

'Do you want to tell me about it?'

You're joking.

'Cameron?'

No reply.

'Cameron – what were you doing out there to-night?' Failure, Pascale thought, total failure. Hadn't she promised herself not to ask?

There was an audible sigh. 'I told you,' Cameron said. 'I was talking to Inuluk.'

'Bit late for a conversation, wasn't it?'

'Middle of the night,' said Cameron. 'Middle of the day. What's the difference here? It's all just endless daylight.'

Not endless. That's what Inuluk had said. Not endless. *Sometimes so dark . . .*

'Cameron –'

'She told me about the storm and the baseball players.'

Which is when Pascale finally admitted to herself that she was as wide awake as he was. She turned over to face him. 'Oh – when the three whalers died?'

'Three whalers and two Inuvialuit. One of them was her great-grandfather.'

'Oh – I'm sorry.'

'And what happened killed her great-grandmother. Although she would have died anyway. Of the flu. Like you said.'

'Oh,' said Pascale again and then: 'Nothing like living history.'

'Didn't seem like history,' said Cameron. 'Not when she was telling it. Seemed like just yesterday.'

'That's what living history is,' said Pascale.

'No, you don't understand.' And suddenly Cameron was sitting bolt upright on the bed. 'When she was telling the story, just for a second, it was almost as if I could hear the storm. Feel the cold of it. Actually on my skin. Under it. And I thought I should feel sorry. Sorry for the people who died, only I didn't. Not at all. I just felt excited. Like – how extraordinary – you could be alive one minute and dead the next. Just like that.'

It was then that Pascale, in the depths of the never dark, fervently wished she'd let Cameron bring his computer.

65

It was the morning and Inuluk realised she hadn't slept. Wasn't it supposed to be her grandmother who never slept? She turned to look at Atka. Atka was staring up at the hill. Inuluk followed her gaze, saw the beautiful snow-white bird.

'*Ukpik*,' Inuluk cried. '*Ukpik*'s on the hill!'

'Yes,' said Atka. 'It is my time – at last.'

'Oh Grandmother, you can't leave me. You can't!'

'All things which begin must also end,' said Atka. 'You know that.'

'But I'm not ready,' cried Inuluk.

'On the contrary,' said Atka. 'You are more than ready.' She paused. 'And I am very tired, Inuluk.'

'What about the task?' asked Inuluk. 'What about Cameron?'

'I think he will finish his own journey now.'

'No!'

'He's seen the tracks,' said Atka. She paused again. 'And so have you. You know where they lead.'

'I'll stop him,' said Inuluk. 'I'll stop him following them!'

'Will you?' said Atka. 'I'm not sure you will.'

'You're scaring me,' Inuluk said.

'To fear is good, remember?' Atka stood up. 'Goodbye now, child.' And she turned her back and began to walk.

Walk away.

'Goodbye?' cried Inuluk. 'Goodbye!'

Atka did not turn. Not for a moment. She just, very slowly, very deliberately, continued on her way.

'Grandmother!'

I'll follow her, thought Inuluk wildly, run up the hill after her, catch her, pull her, haul her back.

But there on the hill was *ukpik*. He shook his snowy feathers and Inuluk never moved.

'Will I see you again?' Inuluk heard her voice stretch, thin across the tundra.

So maybe Atka didn't hear her granddaughter or maybe she did hear and kept on walking anyway. Over the hill and on, on towards the shoreline.

The prints she left were *pisugtoq*'s.

66

Pascale was clattering about making breakfast in the ante-room. Cameron, who felt as though he hadn't slept at all, got out his Flipcam, scrolled through to the hummock and checked one more time.

No Inuluk.

The battery was showing low. He would soon have to have the generator conversation with his mother. And that made him realise that he hadn't charged his iPod. In fact, he hadn't even thought about his iPod. For days. DAYS. And it was weeks (was it weeks?) since he'd last thought about his computer. Or his phone. For that matter, he'd even stopped thinking about the gun. Everything that he had always thought important – just vanished away. Was he going mad? He shook his head, shook away the thought. *Concentrate, Cameron,* he told himself.

'Star Date . . .' he began. What was the date? When he'd powered up the machine for the first time, he'd been asked to enter the date and time but he just hadn't bothered, been too impatient to make his first recording. At home, such things as times and dates were never more than a click away: they were on your phone, your computer, the TV. You could always enter them later.

'Star Date . . .' Cameron began again. Perhaps the date didn't matter. What was a date after all? Some man-made construction.

'Morning, Tom,' he continued.

It was the morning. It had to be the morning because his mother was making breakfast.

'How would you feel, Tom, if – if you didn't know the answer to everything?'

Because that's what it boiled down to, didn't it? That's what was on his mind this star-date morning.

At home there seemed to be answers to pretty much everything. And if you didn't know the answer, you could always find it out. You could go on the net. You could Google a trillion trillion answers in 0.4 seconds. But here – here you had the sense that there might be something, something monumentally important that you were missing. That you didn't know and never would know. It might be as simple as whether it was night – or day. Or perhaps whether there was a terrible storm – or no storm at all. Or even whether you were actually alive or . . .

'Fancy coming to the cove this morning?' Pascale broke brightly into Cameron's reverie. She had a tray of cereal and hot coffee. 'I could really use some help with the old slump measuring.'

'Sorry,' said Cameron, stuffing the Flipcam under his pillow. 'Prior engagement.'

'I'd really like it if you came,' Pascale said, bringing up a crate and setting Cameron's mug and bowl down in front of him. 'I've been thinking about what Dad said. Quality time. I think – maybe it could be good for us.'

'Thing is,' said Cameron, 'I've got a date with a bear.'

'Not funny,' said Pascale.

'Not a joke,' said Cameron. 'Inuluk found bear prints last night.'

'What!' said Pascale.

'Polar bear prints, to be exact.'

'Wrong time of year,' said Pascale quickly. 'We've been through this. Unless the bear was lost of course. Or he was extremely hungry.'

'Not a him,' said Cameron, taking a hot mouthful of coffee. 'A her. It was a she-bear Inuluk dreamed.'

'Oh,' said Pascale hearing the relief in her own voice. 'A dream.'

'Does that mean you don't think dreams can ever be real?' Cameron asked.

'Correct.'

'Well, I'm not sure you're right about that,' said Cameron.

'I do have about three hundred years of post-Enlightenment science on my side,' said Pascale.

'I'd like to look into the eyes of a real live polar bear,' said Cameron. 'I mean – imagine what a bear could tell you.'

'I think you'd find there was a language barrier,' said Pascale.

Cameron ignored her. 'And they're not going to be around much longer are they?'

'Correct,' said Pascale, 'at least as far as polars are

concerned. Brown bears should make it through.'

'Not the same,' said Cameron.

'Wrong,' said Pascale. 'Genetically speaking, polars and browns are pretty much identical.'

'Tell me,' said Cameron.

'Tell you?' He never ever asked her to tell him anything. Pascale felt her heart give a distinctly unscientific flutter. *Tell me!* 'Well,' she said, 'about 200,000 years ago we reckon there were only brown bears. But due to glacier movements some brown bears got cut off from their more southerly neighbours. And it was these bears that evolved into polars.'

'So,' said Cameron slowly, 'if the permafrost does melt, and all the sea-ice, it doesn't matter because the polars will just evolve back into brown bears again?'

'Ah – no, there's a hitch, I'm afraid,' said Pascale. 'You see evolution is a very slow process and warming – well, that's happening very fast. I'd give polars thirty or forty years at the outside.'

Cameron put down his coffee. 'And what would you give Inuluk?'

67

'I'm sorry?' said Pascale. Cameron had seemed so calm, thoughtful even. And now? It was as if a switch had been thrown.

'If Inuluk doesn't keep up,' said Cameron. His eyes were suddenly blazing 'If the world's moved on and her people haven't?'

'I'm not sure this operates at a personal level, Cameron,' Pascal said carefully. 'Although it's certainly an interesting question as to what it's possible or worthwhile to preserve.'

'Worthwhile to preserve!' Cameron exclaimed.

'After all,' Pascale said, reasonably enough, 'we don't mourn the passing of the dinosaurs, do we?'

Cameron jumped up, all agitation. 'And you're saying what? Inuluk's a dinosaur? Had her day?'

'If things disappear from the planet,' said Pascale, refusing to rise, 'you have to ask yourself *what will be lost*? That's all.'

'That's all!' said Cameron. 'Like you could find it all again with your lists and your maps and your measuring rods!'

And that did it. Poked her where it hurt. Fury and disappointment surged through her. 'Oh, sorry,' she said. 'I thought we were having a rational discussion.'

'You know, Mum,' said Cameron, pushing past her, 'you look at loads of stuff. All the time you're looking,

looking through your spyglass, but you know what? I don't think you see anything at all.' He grabbed his anorak.

'Where are you going?' said Pascale. 'Where are you going now?'

'Over to the dark side,' said Cameron.

'Cameron . . .' she called.

But cabin door had already slammed.

68

It was the second night in a row that Inuluk hadn't slept. She'd spent her time on the bear tracks. Starting at the beach, she'd worked her way slowly back to the hill, obliterating the prints one by one. Where they were shallow, she'd scuffed them with her feet, mussing the soil. Where they were deeper, she'd got down on her knees and worked with her hands. She'd smoothed over the indentations, scratched out the claw-marks. She was still down on her knees, intent on her business, when Cameron found her.

'Hi!' he said.

'Oh.' She leapt to her feet, brushed soil from her hands. 'Hi.'

'What are you doing?' asked Cameron.

'Nothing,' she said. 'What are you doing?'

'I'm going on a bear hunt,' he said. '*Gonna catch a big one!*'

'No!' she cried.

'Look, Inuluk . . .' He paused – stared at her very hard.

'Yes?' The staring was odd. As if he wished to commit every part of her – her face, her body – to memory, as though he doubted her existence or thought she might just suddenly disappear.

'Yes?' she said again.

He shook his head, finished with whatever thought

was in his brain. 'I'm really sorry about last night,' he said. 'Sorry about – you know, your great-grandparents and that.'

'Oh,' said Inuluk. 'It was a long time ago.'

'I know,' said Cameron. 'But some things don't change, do they?'

There was something wounded about this remark and Cameron began to pace a bit, fidget, so Inuluk indicated the tundra as you might do a chair, inviting him to sit, to be still. And he did sit. She sat too, beside him but not too close and then she waited.

'Time's supposed to heal,' Cameron said. 'That's what they say, isn't it? But – some things just to go on hurting.'

'Like with your parents?' she asked.

'How can you know that?' he burst out.

'I have eyes, Cameron,' she said. 'And ears.'

Cameron picked a strand of cottongrass, began shredding it. 'I don't want to care,' he said. 'Most of the time I don't care . . .'

'Yes, you do,' said Inuluk. 'And your mother, she cares too. Cares about you. Loves you.'

'Loves me?' Cameron exclaimed. 'I'm not sure she's ever said so.'

'No one's an island, Cameron. You, your parents, London, Qikiqtaruk, the whales, the guillemots, the living . . . the dead. We're all connected. If one moves, we all move.'

There was a short silence in which a bird sang.

'You know, Inuluk, I've never been able to speak to anyone – the way I seem to be able to speak to you.'

'And it's the same for me,' she said, feeling herself flush, but she still carried on. 'As if, before you came, I was only . . . half-alive, like one of Qikiqtaruk's flowers in winter. All curled up under the snow. And now – the summer has arrived.'

She waited to see if he would laugh but he didn't.

'I don't know what to say,' he admitted. 'Cameron O'Connor, lost for words!'

And then they both laughed.

69

After the laughter there was another silence.

Cameron didn't normally like silences. They made him feel uncomfortable, so he usually jumped into them, often with both feet. But sitting here on the tundra, amid the white cottongrass, was different.

I could sit here for ever, he thought, surprising himself.

So he sat and, as he sat, the world came into different focus. The monotonic brown tundra dissolved beneath his gaze, so he felt that he wasn't just sitting on a hill among a mass of flowers but among a thousand, thousand particular flowers. He could see (so he thought) each individual bloom: the separate petals, the different greens of their stems, their hairs and filaments. And then there were the insects. A gossamer-winged butterfly flew past him to perch on a purple spire of Arctic lupin. He watched it fold its sky-blue wings as it landed to reveal a soft grey undercarriage. Next came a spider, an *Aranea* (his mother would have known) with its bulbous orange belly. It made a sudden lunge towards a blow fly. The blow fly was tiny but Cameron suddenly felt that he could see not just the insect's shining lime-green carapace but also its huge blood-red eyes. I wonder, Cameron thought slowly, what it would be like to look out through those eyes?

'So Grandmother was right.' It was Inuluk who finally spoke.

'What about?'

'Stories,' said Inuluk. 'Grandmother says that when you tell your stories, and people actually listen, hear you – that's when you really exist.'

Her smile was translucent.

'You know, Inuluk,' Cameron said, 'I'd really like to meet your grandmother.'

The smile darkened a little.

'Do you think she'd like to meet me?' he couldn't help adding.

'Grandmother's gone,' said Inuluk.

'Gone?' said Cameron. 'Gone where?'

'With the bear,' said Inuluk.

'Oh,' said Cameron. 'Well, never mind.' He stood up. 'All we have to do is follow the tracks and we'll find her then.'

'What tracks?' said Inuluk, far too quickly.

'The bear tracks, of course!' Cameron went over to the place at the bottom of the hill where he remembered putting his hand in the bear-print the previous day.

The soil had been kicked over, scattered.

There were other signs of soil disturbance too, not least at the nearby spot where he had seen her kneeling.

'You – you did this,' he said, looking back at her. 'Didn't you? That's what you were doing when I arrived!'

'Just soil,' said Inuluk, 'shifting. You know how the soil shifts here.'

'You're lying,' Cameron exclaimed.

'What makes you think that?'

'Because you're not very good at it,' said Cameron. 'You've never done it before have you?'

'No,' said Inuluk, simply. 'Well, only about the guillemots. But you still can't go. You can't follow the tracks.'

'Why not?'

'Because it's dangerous.' Inuluk was standing up now.

'But that's the whole point,' said Cameron. 'Isn't it? *Kappia, irksi, il* –'

'*Ilira,*' said Inuluk.

'Yes, *ilira*. Alive one moment and dead the next,' said Cameron. 'That's how you people live.'

'No,' said Inuluk.

'I know where the tracks lead,' said Cameron. 'They lead to the shore. That's what you said last night.'

'This is an island,' said Inuluk. 'There are many shores.'

'But the tracks,' insisted Cameron. 'You pointed that way – over the hill.' He followed his own finger and his eye was caught by a slight movement on the tundra. 'Where that – that bird is.' It was the bird he'd seen before. The bird with the powerful, snow-white wings.

'*Ukpik,*' said Inuluk.

'*Ukpik*?' said Cameron.

'The snowy owl.'

'I thought it was an owl!'

'When *ukpik* comes to the hill,' said Inuluk, 'she brings death.'

'Death?' repeated Cameron.

'Yes,' said Inuluk. 'That's what Grandmother says.'

'And is Grandmother always right?' Cameron asked.

No one had ever asked Inuluk this question before, but then they hadn't had too. Of course Grandmother was always right.

'I don't know,' Inuluk said slowly. 'I mean yes, of course. Except' – she paused – 'perhaps about you.'

'Me?' said Cameron.

'Yes. Grandmother thinks you'll never understand,' said Inuluk. 'About the Island. About how . . . when you tread heavily in your world you also tread in ours. She thinks you're just like all the other *Qallunaat*.'

Cameron looked at her intently. 'And am I?' he asked.

'No!' said Inuluk. 'At least – I don't think so. But . . .' She paused. Now Grandmother had gone the island, the whole island, it depended on her. 'I can't be sure,' she finished.

Cameron spread his arms wide. 'So teach me,' he said, 'take me on the journey.'

'What journey?'

'You know perfectly what journey,' said Cameron

impatiently. 'The journey to the ice, the journey to see the bear!'

'No,' said Inuluk.

'Either you take me or I'll go by myself.'

'You can't,' she said.

'Can't I?' Cameron said. 'I could just walk straight over that hill. Do you want me to walk over the hill, Inuluk? Right past that snowy owl?'

'You're not being fair,' she said.

'Fair?' Cameron exclaimed. 'What's fair got to do with anything? Come on, Inuluk, admit it – everything's been leading to this moment. The Raven story, the burial ground, the dreams which are true, the storm that gives you goosebumps even if it isn't there. I want to go, Inuluk. I want to know what it is that you know.'

'No.'

'Fine,' said Cameron. 'Have it your own way.'

Have it your own way.

Your own way.

And that chance remark afforded Cameron an unexpected insight.

70

'It's not about the tracks,' said Cameron. 'Is it?'

'I'm sorry?' said Inuluk.

'Any more than finding the graveyard for your people,' continued Cameron, 'was about looking on the map.'

'I don't understand,' said Inuluk.

'Yes, you do,' said Cameron. 'You and your people, you don't do things like us, you do them – *your own way*. Like the graveyard. I mean, it was right beneath our feet only I couldn't see it because I wasn't looking in the right place. Or rather, I wasn't looking for the right thing, yes?'

Inuluk kept quiet.

'Like, like – the sky!' Cameron continued. 'I mean look at it – way up there, way, way out of reach. But suppose I looked a different way. Suppose I took my thumb and my forefinger and made a little circle just like this.' And he made such a circle with the finger and thumb of his right hand. 'And then suppose I look through this new view-finder, then there it is!'

'What?' said Inuluk.

'The sky!' Said Cameron. 'The whole sky, I've got it in my hand. I'm holding the whole dome of the universe in the palm of my hand. Well, between my thumb and finger anyway. I'm seeing things *in a different light*. That's it, isn't it? It's about looking, about how you look? Yes? And maybe also about how you listen.' And as soon as he said the word *listen* his dream broke in, in fact it cascaded, and there he was again with the bubbles of the moving sea cod bursting against his flank and sediment on the ocean floor shifting beneath him and the whale halfway around the world singing a welcome.

'And dreaming,' said Cameron, realising. 'It's also about dreaming. Looking and listening and dreaming. I'm right, aren't I? Tell me I'm right!'

But he didn't wait for her to speak because it was all tumbling out of him now. 'The storm. That's what happened with the storm, isn't it? You brought that storm. You! It's coming, you said. And I couldn't hear it, not at first. And then I listened and there it was, I could hear it too. So if we wanted to go to the ice, find your grandmother, I don't even think we'd have to move. I think we could just stand here and bring it all to us. Yes?'

'No.'

'Why do you keep saying "no"? Why did you show me all this stuff if you didn't want me to know it, use it? Because that's really what you've been doing all this time. Teaching me stuff. Giving me *lessons*!'

'No,' said Inuluk. 'No, no, no.'

'Yes,' said Cameron. 'Yes, yes, YES. So now I'm going to do it, have a go. Bring the wind by listening and then maybe the bear!'

'No – never the bear.'

'But the wind,' said Cameron, delighted, 'yes. You just said so!'

So, with his eyes wide open, Cameron O'Connor started to look and listen and dream.

71

Not very far away, in Thetis Bay, Dr Pascale O'Connor was photographing a thaw slump. Looking at the ice wedge in the headwall and the deformation of the adjacent soil, her mind turned to the glacial origins of the island – and also her breakfast conversation with Cameron.

You have to ask yourself – what will be lost.

And no, of course she didn't expect to be able to find it all with her lists and her maps and her measuring rods (and how irritating of him to be able to press this button of hers so easily) but there was something new that occurred to her as she looked at this soil which had been pushed around by a glacier in the last ice age. It was about the cycles of things, how everything that rises, falls again. And how, when one considered life not in terms of months and years or even centuries, but in terms of thousands of years, millions of years – one saw a different picture, a bigger pattern.

Put simply, it was peaks and troughs. After each ice age there was always a warm spell (quite a long warm spell) and then the ice came again. That's how it was, how it had always been. Highs and lows marked on a graph. And it was like this, she mused, not just in geography and geology but also in human culture, in civilisation itself. Different peoples and nations ruled the world for a time – and then they passed into history.

The conquering Romans became simple Italians. The marvellous British Empire faded into commonwealth. Peoples rose, peoples fell.

And. And?

And therefore (Dr Pascale O'Connor thought at Thetis Bay), if humans were to devastate the planet, making it uninhabitable for themselves (she checked herself – thinking, *at least my work contributes some necessary data to start this conversation*) then all that would happen would probably be that another species would rise to fill the gap. A species such as – she looked down and happened to spot a red and orange beetle – the *Endomychidae*. And if this *Endomychidae* – or Handsome Fungus Beetle – didn't mind the warming, if he and his kind were impervious to higher temperatures and rising sea-levels and just went on happily making more Handsome Fungus Beetles – then who was to say that was wrong?

The Empire of Man followed by the Empire of Beetles.

Just another peak and trough, thought Dr Pascale O'Connor, in the turning of the world.

72

Cameron held himself very still. His feet were firmly planted on the green tundra earth at the bottom of the hill. But his mind – that was loosening. The world around him began to blur. Or maybe he was blurring, becoming just a little closer to the things which surrounded him.

Like the wind.

It was only a light flutter at first, a whisper. It ruffled and rustled the purple spires of the Arctic lupins, it brushed the underwings of butterflies, it kissed his face. Just as it kissed the face of the blow fly with the blood-red eyes. A warm, summer breeze, but one which had travelled with the ocean and which (as Cameron listened harder, loosened more) seemed to carry a deeper, rougher note.

'There,' Cameron cried. 'There! Can you hear it?'

Inuluk could hear it, of course she could. And she could hear beyond and through it, right back to the beginning, to *sila,* the substance of life, the breath that circulates into and out of every living being. The breath that is both the whisper of breezes and the flesh-stripping power of a storm. *Sila* that cannot be created or destroyed but is simply recycled, so that as one creature dies another takes its breath and lives on. The breath one uses when one makes a word in one's mouth and which, as the ancestors' taught, gives that named thing life.

Yes, Inuluk heard all this.

She was also aware of the slither of ice in the winter Cameron was bringing. The coming of a wind which would swirl and howl and hollow things out. And beneath that wind – whipped by it – the open sea.

Cameron heard the sea too, but only like you do in a shell, in the cup of your ear. Softly, far away. It was a very different sensation from the one he'd had when he was a whale and heard with his whole body. If I want to conjure the ocean, he thought, perhaps I need to do as the whale does, be as the whale is. Listen with the hollow of my bones.

So he shut his eyes, trying to tune his body to the faraway sounds. And, gradually those sounds became louder, nearer. He could feel the rock and swell of the waves.

'Told you,' said Cameron. 'Told you, told you, told you!'

'Grandmother says,' said Inuluk angrily, 'that when she was born, the ice came to the shore. Even in summer. Ice fast to the coast and further out, pack ice.'

'Oh listen!' cried Cameron. But he wasn't listening to Inuluk. He was hearing the mist of the freezing days from the moon (though he didn't know it) of *Itartoryuk*. Of November, when the *tuglu* – the sea ice – of the previous month begins to thicken.

'The bear needs the ice as a platform,' said Inuluk. 'To hunt from.'

'I can smell it,' shouted Cameron. 'Smell the ice.'

And he could now, the chill of it in his nostrils and, behind his dimmed eyes, the tiniest of ice crystals were forming, minuscule six-point stars of glass. A thousand of them. A million of them. The beginning of an ice sheet.

'But if the sea's too warm,' said Inuluk, 'the ice breaks up. The bear has nowhere to stand. She can't hunt. That's why she sometimes comes inland. Angry. Starving.'

The ice was thickening. Or should have been thickening. Or perhaps once had thickened, long ago. Inuluk heard the muffled sounds of the ice as it gathered in Cameron's imagination, as it lay and floated and moved with the tides. And she heard the first of the cracks, like a whip. Cameron didn't hear the whip cracks, not at first. He didn't hear them until they were as loud as pistol shots.

'What's that?' he cried.

'Ice,' said Inuluk. 'You've brought ice, Cameron. Only it's your ice. *Qallunaat* ice. So it's fracturing.'

Cameron opened his eyes.

73

At Thetis Bay, Dougie, the Park Ranger, had joined Pascale. They had been working together in silence for half an hour or more before Dougie said: 'I thought you said your son was coming today.'

Pascale was thinking about massive ice melt, she was wondering about ground subsidence and the possible development of new Arctic ponds and wetlands.

'Found himself some people from the Generational Project to play with,' she said.

'Generational Project?' asked Dougie.

'Yes. You know, the grandparent-grandchild thing. The one they always run at about this time of year.'

'Only not this year,' said Dougie.

Pascale quit what she was doing, looked up. 'I'm sorry?'

'It's been getting more and more difficult to find the elders,' said Dougie. 'Every year there are fewer and fewer of them left. The people who really knew the island. Know the old ways. So it was cancelled this year.'

'Cancelled?'

'Yes.'

'But there's this girl,' said Pascale. 'She's been telling Cameron all the stories. About the storm and the whalers and – Inuluk, her name's Inuluk.'

'Inuluk?' Dougie tipped his head to one side.

'Yes.'

'No one around here calls their child Inuluk anymore,' said Dougie.

'They don't?'

'No. Not since the last child of that name died here, anyway.'

'Died here?' said Pascale, her heart giving an unexpected jump.

'Yes. Out on the ice. Beneath the ice.'

Pascale's face must have not been liking this answer because Dougie added: 'But that was many moons ago, of course.'

74

Inuluk was standing on the edge of Cameron's ice sheet. 'What do you see, Cameron?' she asked.

'Nothing,' he replied. 'Just dark. It's all dark.' The sea, the sky, he could make nothing out. There was just one blackness.

'Look harder,' said Inuluk.

He looked again, tried to focus and gradually his eyes adjusted. The dark broke up a little, he could see pale lines, grey fractures. Then the pistol-shot noise came again: from the right of him, from the left, from behind him. 'What's happening?' Cameron cried.

'I told you. It's just the ice breaking apart,' said Inuluk. 'Because of the warming. Do you see the floes?'

'No.'

'Look again.'

Cameron looked. The sky had divided from the sea. And spread in front of him, spread towards that slim horizon, was a heave of dark things. He spun around. They were behind him too. 'Dark,' he said, 'dark patches . . .'

'Yes,' said Inuluk. 'Dark ice floating on a dark sea. Feel it now, Cameron. Feel it under your feet.'

And he did. Almost lost his balance as he realised he was standing on one of those dark, dark patches. He wobbled, nearly fell. 'It isn't stable!' he shouted.

'*Kappia,*' said Inuluk. 'The fear of danger. Some of

the large pieces, they're metres thick. But some of the smaller pieces, they're thinner, drift faster. I think this is a smaller piece, Cameron. The one we're standing on.'

Cameron felt the ice move beneath him with the swell of the sea. 'You're joking,' he said, though he knew perfectly well she wasn't.

'If you want to find the bear,' Inuluk continued, 'you must do as the bear does, Cameron. Jump the floes.'

'But Inuluk,' wailed Cameron. 'The bear can swim!'

'Can't you swim, Cameron?'

'I don't remember you saying to bring trunks!'

'Jump, Cameron,' said Inuluk. 'If you want to meet the bear, then jump.'

Cameron looked at the nearest ice floe, saw how it floated on the ocean, freezing water slop, slop, slopping against its edges. He also looked at the gap. The gap of black, swelling water which divided him from that floe. It was six feet, seven feet maybe.

'I can't,' he said.

'Jump,' said Inuluk.

'But they're moving,' said Cameron. 'Look at them move.'

It was true, the sea was a pitiless landscape of moving ice.

Six feet, seven feet of black water between each treacherous floe.

Nine.

Some of the floes looked pack-ice thick, some glass thin. But you couldn't really tell because the colour of their mirror blackness, their density seemed to change as they were dragged back and forth in time with the tide.

'How do I know it will take my weight?' asked Cameron of the floe nearest to him.

'How does the bear?' said Inuluk. 'How did I, when I jumped that last ever time?'

'When you jumped?' repeated Cameron.

'When I was a child,' said Inuluk. 'Your age.'

'You're still my age,' cried Cameron.

'Jump – they called,' said Inuluk.

Jump, Inuluk, jump.

75

Inuluk remembered.

Memories suddenly welling and washing against her.

It was the winter the hunters – Krinrartak, Kreviunak and Ovayuak – were caught by the opening of the ice fields. The sea ice always broke in the same places; the hunters knew the tides and the currents and the months of its happening. But that year, the break-up had been earlier than usual, a lead of black water appearing quite suddenly. And the hunters were on the wrong side of that lead, found themselves cut adrift on a huge platform of ice that was floating inexorably out to sea. Inuluk remembered how it was her quick-witted grandfather who had saved them, using the ice itself, a much smaller piece which had also broken off. He used it as a boat, paddled the ice floe out to the hunters, brought them back safely.

When the story had been told – and re-told – the elders had laughed.

Call themselves hunters and they don't know the ice!

The secret of survival in the Arctic Ocean? Stay on the boat!

Which is why no one stopped the children going down to the shore to learn about the ice. Just as no one took a hunting knife from the hands of a toddler. How was a child to grow into an adult if he didn't find out what was useful to know?

MASALLAK

snow that makes
good snowballs

It was May, under the moon of *Tigmiyikvik*, the time when the ducks and the geese return from the South. There was still ice fast to the shore but further out the pack ice was moving.

Come, said Oyangin.

Come, said Putugor.

They'd gone together. Hadn't told anyone where they were going and no one had asked.

It was warm enough to be wearing just an outer parka, not the inner jacket of caribou with the fur turned towards the skin. So too with the *kamiak*, her caribou-skin boots, she had chosen just one layer. Put no wolverine fur about her face. But she did pull on her waterproof sealskin overshoes, after all, they were going to jump on the ice.

And then they walked together, the excitement building. But silently. They said nothing to each other as they made their way over the shore-fast ice.

What was there to say?

They arrived later than they had intended. The orange of the moon sparkling on the ice; large slow-motion, wet snowflakes unexpectedly falling. *Masallak* – the sort of snow which is good for snowballs.

Sometimes the broken sea ice was jagged, ragged with the winds and the pressure ridges of drifting. That day it was flat, almost as flat as the sea, which was darker by now.

The floes were shining, moon-coloured plates of ice floating on the water.

Putugor was first, he always had to be the first, jumping from the safety of the shore-fast ice to the first of the floes.

Now he laughed.

Now his laughter streamed in the ice-cold air.

Inuluk and Oyangin caught the tail of that laugh and they jumped too, together. Only Oyangin was a little in front and a little heavier.

'Jump,' cried Putugor. 'Jump!'

But the girls were already jumping. They were in mid-air. Or at least Inuluk was, but Oyangin, she had landed and the floe – which looked so icy-calm and moonlit-beautiful, sank a little under the force of her landing feet.

So when Inuluk alighted, hardly a moment later, the plate of ice was slightly dipped beneath the surface of the ocean and Inuluk's feet landed in water. Arctic water, which her sealskin overshoes repelled. But the overshoes could not repel the lurch and dip of the floe as it adjusted to the children's weight, Inuluk's particularly.

So Inuluk felt herself slide and there was nothing to hang onto.

The slide destabilised the floe and it was as much as Oyangin could do to stay upright herself as she saw Inuluk disappear into the water. Black water. Freezing water.

The shock of the cold was immediate, punching. Inuluk gasped, taking a whole chestful of water as she

SINKING

went under for the first time. But she rose and sputtered, stunned, astonished. The bare skin of her face and hands pulled tight, the sub-zero sea a thousand needles in her. And then she was under again, her clothes sodden and heavy, dragging her ever deeper. And she wanted to gasp again, gasp for air, but she was under, under the water, under the ice. The black above her was solid.

It had no edge.

She fought with her hands, flailed, her lungs bursting. Where was the edge? Up, she was up, but trapped, trapped beneath the ice and the ice was moving and there wasn't much time.

And if Putogor and Oyangin were screaming at her, for her (which they were), then she didn't hear them. And if they were stretching for her (which they were, seeing her dark body move beneath the ice) then those were just empty arms for nothing could reach her.

She was going down.

76

Inuluk was shivering, her whole body shaking so violently that Cameron felt the ice beneath them tremble too.

'The water closed black over my head,' Inuluk cried. 'The ice. *Irksi*. Terror. I couldn't breathe. I couldn't breathe.' And then, standing beside Cameron, pulling herself from the past, she screamed, 'I can't breathe Cameron!'

'Here,' he said instinctively. 'Take my hand.'

But she wouldn't, couldn't, so he reached for her, clasped her hand in his. And he had a strange feeling that he'd held her hand before (or she'd held his) though maybe that was just in a dream.

Or a dream of a dream.

'We'll jump. We'll do it together,' he said. 'Jump, Inuluk.'

And so they did. They jumped together, they flew across the dark water and landed together on a moon of ice.

'Wow!' said Cameron. 'Wow. Amazing!'

'You did it!' said Inuluk and she didn't seem to be shivering any more.

'You did it!' said Cameron.

And then he jumped again. He just couldn't help it. His feet were springs, his heart a burst of surprise, of exhilaration.

And she followed him as if the floes were giant lily pads and they were Arctic frogs, creatures light on their long, strong legs.

'Can't catch me,' shouted Cameron.

'Can so,' said Inuluk, only half a floe behind him.

And of course there was laughter. How could there not be? Laughter like kisses in the cold air.

Again and again they jumped and chased and laughed. Sometimes he was ahead, sometimes she was. They teased and surprised each other, jumping distances they never knew they had it in them to jump. Eventually, exhausted, Cameron flung himself full-stretch on the ice. He didn't even feel the cold.

'You know, Inuluk,' he said, 'I don't think I've ever felt like this before.'

'*Nuannapoq,*' said Inuluk, coming to land beside him, her face more sparkling than the ice.

'What?' said Cameron.

'Our word for it,' said Inuluk. '*Nuannapoq*. The extravagant pleasure of being alive.' And something healed in her then.

'I don't think we have that word in our language,' said Cameron.

'My language,' said Inuluk, joyfully. 'My people's language.'

'That might be lost,' said Cameron.

'No, never.' said Inuluk. 'Because you'll remember, won't you Cameron?'

'For ever,' he replied. 'For ever and ever.'

NUANNAPOQ

77

How long did they lie beside each other on that glittering ocean?

Long enough for the wind to drop and the sudden silence bring the sound of their own heartbeats. Long enough for the ice to move and the birds to come, a million, million chattering birds. Or so Cameron thought.

'Where are they?' he cried.

'What?' said Inuluk.

'The birds, of course.'

'That's not birds,' said Inuluk, 'that's icebergs.'

'Icebergs?' This was not the last of the things Cameron heard or saw that day that he would not previously have believed.

'Where?' he asked.

'Behind you.' Inuluk pointed at an entire cliff face of ice, steep walls sheer into the sea. Cameron had never seen anything so monumental, one berg behind the next, stretching into a mountain range of ice. Bright white against the sky but also grey, the colour of doves and smoke.

The bergs drifted with a kind of massive silence and yet he could still hear their internal chatterings.

'How can they sound like that?' he said.

'How can they look like that?' said Inuluk.

'Cathedrals,' said Cameron. 'Cathedrals of ice.' Because that's how they seemed to him suddenly:

towering testaments to the glory of God. Cameron had never thought much about God before. But there was something so colossal about these bergs, so majestic and so perfectly indifferent to him, that he had a glimpse of the sacred, felt as though he'd stumbled into the imagination of the divine.

'Fallen pieces of the moon,' said Inuluk, who felt a lingering sadness looking at these remote giants, these huge, broken fragments of the Arctic floating away – to what?

'Oh and look – there!' called Cameron.

At water level, where the surf pounded, there were grottos, caverns and ice bridges, and, higher up, columns and spires. There were old fractures, new fractures, milk-blue melt waters and there also was the wave. A wave over a mile long, a huge curved back wall of water – totally frozen, frozen in the act of falling. A graceful curve of glass blue with a huge fringe of frozen white spray. Water falling but never fallen, suspended in mid-air.

'How is that even possible, Inuluk?'

'Everything is possible,' said Inuluk.

'Oh, Inuluk,' said Cameron. 'I think we've finally done it. Arrived!'

Which is when they heard the noise. Faraway it could have been the sound of an iceberg calving, an immense slab of ice shearing from the mother block. Nearer to, it might just have signified the powerful, resonant footfall of a bear.

78

Dr Pascale O'Connor was not a superstitious woman. She did not believe in omens or portents or vague feelings in the pit of one's stomach. But Dougie's story had unnerved her. She'd gone over the facts in her head a number of times and, of course, there were explanations. So why did the disquiet remain?

She began again:

1. Cameron had never actually mentioned the Generational Project.

2. It was she who had mentioned the Generational Project, jumped to the conclusion (jumping to conclusions was not generally advised by the scientific community) that if there was a child on the island and a grandmother they must be on the project.

3. Just because the Generational Project had been cancelled this year it didn't mean that *one particular* grandmother couldn't have come to the island to show things to *her own* granddaughter.

4. However, 1 to 3 did not explain why she, Pascale, had never actually seen the child despite (apparently) more than one opportunity to do so.

5. Therefore . . .

Therefore what?

Therefore the vague feeling in the pit of her stomach. Therefore a strange vision behind her eyes. The impossibly stupid and irrational picture of this one particular grandmother as a bear.

A polar bear.

'Dougie,' Dr O'Connor said, 'have you any reason to believe there are bears on the island this summer?'

'No,' said Dougie.

'Good,' said Dr Pascale O'Connor. 'Good. That's all right, then.' And she bent back down as if she was concentrating on her work.

79

Cameron had no doubt what the noise was. After all, he'd heard it before – if only in a dream. This powerful, rhythmic noise was the pad of a bear.

'I don't see it!' he cried, spinning.

'Fear in the bone,' said Inuluk, feeling an unexpected spiking of fur on the back of her neck.

'Where is it, Inuluk?'

'Fear in the blood,' said Inuluk. Her nail-beds were pricking. The way they might have done if she had been born with claws not fingernails. 'I'm sorry, Cameron.'

Cameron was still wheeling. 'Make it stop, Inuluk. I think I've had enough.' Besides, he realised suddenly, he'd forgotten his bear spray.

'I can't stop it,' said Inuluk. 'Not now. It's the end of the story. *Ilira*. The fear of something you cannot control or predict.' She didn't know exactly why she said this, it seemed more like something her grandmother might say. Which is when the bear appeared.

A huge, golden-white bear standing not ten feet in front of them.

Cameron stood transfixed. 'Raven made polar bear,' he whispered, 'so man would be afraid!'

The bear was standing on its hind legs the way bears do when they are about to attack.

'Awestruck,' said Inuluk. 'So man would be awestruck.'

ILIRA
the fear that
accompanies
awe

'Paws the size of dinner plates,' said Cameron. The sensible thing to do would be to run away. But Cameron was not running away. His eyes seemed locked with the bear's. 'Four rows of razor-sharp teeth . . .'

'*Pisugtoq*,' said Inuluk. The fur on her back was getting more dense and the weight in her legs increasing. She felt there might only be so many more words in her mouth before she could only growl. 'The Great Wanderer,' she said. Her paws thundered the ice in time with the names. 'Ice Bear. Sea Bear. Nanuk. Isbjorn.'

Cameron seemed on auto-pilot, walking as if in slow motion towards the larger of the two bears. Because there were two bears now. One a magnificent old, golden-white bear and the other, a rather more shadowy, paler, younger bear. If Cameron noticed the transformation in Inuluk, he didn't mention it. He was on his own journey now, just as Grandmother had said.

There was something inexorable about the movement of the old bear and the movement of the boy. It was as though there was a string between their eyes, a string getting shorter and shorter every moment, so if you had been looking (and the younger bear was certainly looking) you would have known it was only a matter of time, a very short time, before the two came together. Before the boy – whose flesh looked particularly white and vulnerable – met the paws and claws and jaws of *pisugtoq*. Jaws which had dripped the blood of a thousand former kills.

The young bear looked, but she did not move, did not try to intervene. Because the old bear was always right. Had always been right. The old bear was –

'Lord of the Arctic,' said Inuluk. Only it didn't come out as separate words but as one long snarl as Inuluk, finally, leapt between her grandmother and the boy.

Atka halted. Teeth bared, right paw still raised, she stared down at the young cub. The challenger. Stared this pretender – pretender to the throne of bears and islands and hope – straight in the eye.

And this time, Inuluk held her gaze.

Or, at least she did until the gun went off.

80

Dr Pascale O'Connor had aimed at the eyes. Through the whiff of cordite, she saw something fall.

It was her son.

'Cameron,' she cried. 'Oh my god – Cameron.' Dropping the smoking gun, she flew across the ground to his side. It might have been two yards, or a hundred – her feet never touched the green, tussocky land.

'Cameron!' She was on her knees reaching for him. He was limp, he was heavy, she lifted his head, she cradled it in her lap. 'Speak to me!'

There was a pause (which seemed to last an eternity) and then Cameron said: '*Nuannapoq*.' His voice was otherworldly.

'Oh,' gasped Pascale, 'oh, oh, oh,' and, without a moment's hesitation, she bent right down and kissed that other-worldly head.

'The extravagant pleasure of being alive,' Cameron added.

'Oh yes! You're alive! Thank god. Oh thank God.' Could she really have pointed that gun just beyond where he was standing, pulled the trigger, fired so close? 'I love you, Cameron,' she heard herself saying. 'I love you so much.'

'I saw her mouth,' said Cameron.

'What?'

Cameron pulled away from his mother. 'Not her

MOTHER

teeth but her pale violet mouth. Her grey tongue.'

'Cameron . . .' said Pascale.

But Cameron was up now, he was on his feet. Wild, she thought, he looks wild.

'And I wasn't scared,' Cameron said, 'not at all, not at first. And then I looked in her eyes. Or rather, she looked in mine. They have tiny eyes, polar bears. Tiny pin-pricks of darkness in that great sweep of white. But they were more piercing than the drill that killed the whale. Eyes full of rage and incomprehension. And also beauty, as if she knew a thousand things that I would never know.'

'Cameron . . .' said Pascale.

'And I thought I should speak,' said Cameron. 'Speak to the bear! That she was waiting. But there was nothing in my head – except one word. *Sorry*.'

81

'And then,' said Cameron, 'you shot her.' He paused. The appalling truth finally registering. 'You shot the polar bear.' His mother had shot the polar bear in those pin-prick beautiful eyes!

'No, no, no – hang on,' said Pascale. 'I mean I know I fired the gun and that was stupid, idiotic . . .' And the flashback came then as it would come a thousand times in the future. Cameron standing before a huge polar bear. A bear high on its hind legs, teeth bared, paw raised, just a moment from striking. 'But you know how it is in the light here,' Pascale continued, refusing every one of those pit-of-the-belly fears. 'Reflection. Refraction. Sunlight and ice crystals. Water droplets. Diffraction by airborne particles. It was physics,' said Dr Pascale O'Connor. 'It was a MIRAGE!'

It was the science talking. And the shock. But there would come a time – and not such a distant time either – when Pascale would remember things differently. Would think, in moments of quietness, that perhaps there was more to the island than had met her immediate eye. Perhaps a whole raft of things indeed, that couldn't be measured and known the way she had always measured and known things. Perhaps this is what the near-death of her son taught her. That – and something about love. But all that was in the future.

'And Inuluk,' said Cameron. 'You shot Inuluk!'

'No!' said Pascale. 'I didn't shoot Inuluk. Didn't shoot a bear, didn't shoot Inuluk.'

Cameron was looking about him. He was looking on the tundra for the bodies of a huge bear and a slip of a girl. Or perhaps a huge bear and a slightly smaller bear. Because, he realised suddenly, there'd been another bear, hadn't there? There'd been two bears!

'In fact,' Pascale continued. 'I don't really think there is an Inuluk.'

'No!' said Cameron, though he didn't know if he was denying his mother or the shock of his coming understanding. 'She was here. Right here.'

Yet the only thing that lay about him was hummocky grass. One hummock bigger than the other, but hummocky grass nonetheless.

'That Generation Project,' said Pascale. 'They didn't run it this year. There weren't any elders. There weren't any children.'

'That's just not true!' Cameron cried. And he was crying, almost, or that's what it felt like. Tears pricking in his eyes, his heart lurching in his chest.

Inuluk had stood between him and the bear!

'There's a supply plane coming tomorrow,' said Pascale. 'We'll take it. We'll go home. I'll take a week off work. Two weeks maybe. We'll sort all this out. Have some real time together. You and me.'

'Inuluk,' Cameron called. He was spinning now, turning and turning on the soil of the island. 'Inuluk,' he called again. 'Inuluk!'

But only the birds answered.

Pascale came up close to her son, took him by the wrists. 'Cameron – look at me.'

And he had to.

Look in her pale, frightened eyes.

'It's all right,' said his mother. 'Everything's going to be all right.' And then she seemed to find an inspiration. 'What you need is this!' He felt her reach into the pocket of his anorak, draw out his iPod. 'We'll go back,' she said, clamping on the earphones. 'To civilisation. You'll see.'

And she switched on the machine.

82

The first thing Inuluk saw when she woke was Pascale putting things in Cameron's ears. Though *woke* is not quite the right word for someone recovering from their first transitioning. It was more like moving slowly through a veil of consciousness. Edges blurred for a minute, as Inuluk was neither one thing (bear) nor another (girl).

So this is how it must have felt to grandmother, Inuluk thought.

Grandmother.

And Inuluk would have looked for Atka then but she heard Pascale say 'Come now' to Cameron and she knew there wasn't much time.

So she pulled herself to her Inuit feet.

What she needed to do would only take a moment, though it would be more difficult than she was prepared for.

She moved at the first opportunity, when Pascale went to retrieve the gun. Slipped quietly between mother and son, stood behind Cameron.

Close enough to touch.

And she did touch him, just as she had at the beginning of the journey to Planet Sea, only this time she touched his head, cupped her hands over his ears as if those hands were shells and carried all the sounds of the island in them.

The sounds were only murmurs: the ocean as it washed and sucked at the black soil of Qikiqtaruk's shore; the wind as it came inland with a slither of ice; the long wild, tremolo moan of *urgruk*; the electric snapping of shrimp; the submarine song of a newborn whale calf, the growl and roar of a polar bear.

And she knew Cameron heard these things, even though he had the plugs of the machine in his ears. Because when the wind blew, he bent with it and when the whale calf sang his shoulders laughed and when the polar bear roared the whole of his body trembled.

She held these murmurs close to his head so he would remember. So he would keep his promise '*for ever and ever*' and there would never be a moment when he listened to the music of his people when he didn't also listen to the music of hers.

'Tell your people, Cameron,' she whispered. 'Tell them everything as I have taught it you.'

From a small distance, Pascale saw her son trembling.

'I promise,' said Cameron. 'I swear.'

'Shh,' said Pascale, coming closer. 'Shh. It's OK.' Gun slung over her shoulder now, she pushed past Inuluk (who after all was only a mirage) and put her arm around her son's shoulder. 'Time to go.'

And then they began walking.

Walking away from her.

Just like Grandmother.

And Inuluk had to stand and watch, watch their

backs, Cameron's back in particular. The whole shadowed shape of him walking away and never turning, not looking back.

And she couldn't follow him because, like Grandmother, Cameron was going to a place which was beyond her.

Finally he arrived at a horizon. Cameron outlined against the wide sky. And that's when he stopped. Her heart almost stopped with him. And the island seemed to hold its breath as he finally turned.

Turned to look.

Could he see her at that distance?

Could he see her now she was Guardian?

For she was Guardian. Inuluk knew that now.

Cameron, her heart cried, though she never made a sound.

Cameron looked long and he looked hard.

Scoured all the hills and hummocks of Qikiqtaruk. So perhaps he did see her that one last time. And perhaps, long after he was grown and had children of his own, he remembered that image of the girl standing alone on the island.

That dream of a dream of the first girl he ever loved.

83

A polar bear is not a herd animal. It gives birth to its young and then lets them go. They walk alone.

Inuluk thought this as she tended to Atka, who was neither bear nor old woman. But soil. The soil of the island. And also *sila,* the breath of lichen and crowberry.

So why did Inuluk weep as she tended that soil and inhaled those sweet, sweet scents of Qikiqtaruk? Why were her eyes blinded as she picked up her grandmother's staff and felt its knots beneath her fingers?

The death of an animal is a gift. An animal chooses his own death, chooses the hunter to whom he will submit. That's what Atka had always said. And Atka the bear had chosen the *Qallunaat.* Given herself to her most hated enemy. Submitted. Chosen a death the woman with the gun would never forget. That Cameron would never forget.

'He will tell your stories to the world,' Inuluk said to the sweetened air. 'He will tell his people and the island will live. I know it. For he gave his word. You heard him, didn't you, Grandmother?'

And then Inuluk took the staff and broke it, broke it over her knee. Because she was not her grandmother and never could be.

She marked this place at the bottom of the hill (the hill where *ukpik* had sat) with that stick.

'Graves should be marked,' that's what Cameron had said. Inuluk smiled as she pressed one end of the broken staff into the ground.

Not that this was a grave. For there is no grave in the cycle of things which live and die, and live again in the breath of others. She marked the place only out of respect for Cameron. For his people had a way of doing things too and she wanted to honour that.

Cameron.

Oh – Cameron.

He would think of the island but would he think of her?

She would think of him.

And what might have been if the world had been different.

She shook the thought away. There was a new journey to be undertaken.

She had mussed the tracks, but they were still bright in her memory, she knew the place of each and every one of them. It was nothing to follow the prints over the hill and down to the shore. And so she followed the way of *pisugtoq*, standing upright at first and then dropping to all fours as her fur thickened and her legs strengthened.

She couldn't see her own mouth, but she could taste it, the violet pinkness, the sharp white teeth. Just as she was alert to her weapon-honed claws and her easy, slightly lopsided gait. Her fur was still much whiter than Grandmother's, though near her paws, she noted, there were the first flecks of lemon-yellow.

When she reached the shoreline, she gave a little roar. Just for the pleasure of it. Just for hearing the sound in her throat become sound in the air.

I have not played enough, she thought, as she came to the edge of the sea, and waded into the water.

Well, now she would play, play and swim. Swim in that freezing water and never feel the cold. Dive for kelp, sit by the *aglu* of a seal, wander the Arctic under the moons of *Avunnivik*, of *Nuertovik*, of *Tugluvik*. Travel a thousand miles. A thousand, thousand miles. She felt her paws lift, buoyed by the water, felt them leave the soil of Qikiqtaruk (although that soil continued – Grandmother said – far, far under the ocean) as she streamlined into the sea.

There would be a time for return.

But now the ocean called to her. The open sea and the ice. She would swim for the ice, a hunter at home in her hunting ground. The land of her dreams and belonging, the frozen place to which she had been born.

And – for the time being at least – all would be well.

GUARDIAN

Island – the Director's Cut

So many people have nurtured *Island*. It's a tale of chance remarks, serendipitous meetings – and incredible generosity.

Let me begin at the beginning. The day when Associate Director Anthony Banks rang me up and asked if I'd like to write a play for the National Theatre. There was a silence my end of the phone.

'You're not going turn it down?'

'Well,' I began, 'you think I know how to write a play because of *Feather Boy* the musical and *Knight Crew* the opera – but those were both adaptations of my novels. I've never actually written a play from scratch before.'

'A week,' he said, 'you can have a week to think about it.'

As luck would have it, I spent that week in Morocco visiting old friends – Martin and George Rose. One morning at breakfast, their daughter Frances began talking about a trip the family had made on a previous posting to Canada. They'd travelled with a permafrost scientist to an Arctic island called Herschel. On that bright sunshiny Moroccan terrace, Frances talked of blizzards and whaling boats stuck in ice; of shallow graves and things which should be buried being uncovered; of bear prints in the sand and twenty-four hour daylight. 'A place where I felt,' she continued in a phrase that went straight into my notebook, 'awake for possibilities.'

I returned to England and phoned the theatre. 'There's this Grandmother,' I said, 'and two kids and they're on this island in the middle of nowhere and there's an ice storm and erupting graves and probably a polar bear. And the whole things is full of sounds, wind and waves and icebergs and krill and whale song. What do you think?'

'That you'd better start straight away,' said Mr Banks.

I came to believe the island was a microcosm for the impact of global warming; the graves opening because of the melting of the permafrost. But I needed to get my facts right – on this and many other things. The Canadian scientist the Rose family had travelled to Herschel with was Professor Christopher Burn. A fount of information and kindness, he Skyped and emailed answers to questions as diverse as 'what sort of people become Arctic research scientists?' to 'are there pea pods on Herschel?' For the record, all the scientific information in the book, including the flora and fauna is – to the best of my knowledge – accurate to the island: much of it gleaned from Chris's own wonderful book *Herschel Island: Qikiqtaryuk: A Natural and Cultural history of Yukon's Arctic Island*. (Any errors are mine, obviously.) Two other books also became primary sources and great loves: Hugh Brody's compelling work *The Other Side of Eden*, based on his first-hand experience of living with hunter-gatherers, and *Arctic Dreams* by Barry Lopez, a book of astonishing beauty about Northern landscapes and people.

It didn't seem so very long before I was in a rehearsal room. What a surprising place that was. The creative journeys of a novel and a play are very different. For a novel, you go into a dark, solitary space with a piece of grit to emerge approximately (in my case) eighteen months later with a small pearl. Whatever lustre the pearl has – or doesn't have – is down to you and you alone. You are the king or queen of the dark, solitary space and no one has powers there but you.

Imagine such a queen coming into the rehearsal room and finding a bunch of other creative people there. Nice – but what are they doing in your work space? Imagine such a person having to bring her pearl – when it's still very much a piece of grit – and put it on the table for these other people to inspect. That's what it's like for the novelist turned playwright. Scary. And exhilarating. Because – actually, the people in this room are amazing. Director Adam Penford, interrogating the script line by line. Designer Simon Kenny, bringing new colours and textures – the island sewn together with animal skins. Sound designer Tom Gibbons, making music from sounds you've heard before (breaking ice like pistol shots) and sounds you haven't – the call of seals zapping through water like electronic arrows. And then there are the actors – Rebecca Boey as Inuluk, Jilly Bond as Pascale, James Cooney as Cameron and Anne Kavanagh as Grandmother – each of them breathing full life into your pale, shadowy characters. I nearly left the planet with excitement.

And then it was finally on! It played to packed houses in the Cottesloe, got a rafts of 4-star reviews and toured numerous London schools. And then . . .

It was over.

Done. Dusted. Gone.

Bit of a shock that, for a novelist. You see, we're used to leaving traces. Quite fat 250-page traces.

But I let it go, moved on.

Until, that is, about a year later when there was a sudden flurry of newspaper articles about the melting ice-caps. Five people rang me up in the same week.

'What happened to *Island*?' they asked.

'Well, nothing. Slipped away. Much like the island itself probably will . . .'

'Then write it as a novel,' they said. 'Our young people need that story more than ever. Don't you understand? They have to have the chance to engage with what's going on in the Arctic. Do it. Do it now!'

I realised I still had things to say about the subject. So I began again.

And I fell in love with my characters – again. I also liked the extra space in the book; it allowed me to add in some detail that didn't make it into the play. All in all, I thought I made a pretty good fist of the re-write. The publishing industry disagreed.

'It's too *quiet*,' they said, 'for the current market'.

I'm not sure this particular term has made the *OED* yet but, roughly translated, I think it means: 'this book will not make a shed-load of money'. Leaving aside the fact that if publishers really knew what made money eight of them wouldn't have turned down Harry Potter, they are, in *Island*'s case, probably right. But then I didn't write *Island* to make a shed-load of money. I wrote it because it seemed a story which still needed to be told.

Cue Ursula Le Guin's blistering address to the US National Book Awards last year (available on YouTube) where she talks about the difference between *'the production of a market commodity and the practice of an art'*. She goes on to wonder at us – the writers and creators – *'who let profiteers sell us like deodorant and tell us what to publish and what to write'*. She finishes by demanding, not shed-loads of money – but freedom.

What might this freedom look like for someone like me? To be able to publish what I hope is a powerful, meaningful story in powerful, meaningful language. For young people. Yes – young people. Which is another problem. As well as being 'too quiet', *Island* was also deemed 'too literary' for these apparently lesser mortals. I've felt this chill before. Not least when I was asked to expunge the word 'bonnet' from a previous novel on the basis that no self-respecting twelve-year-old would know such a word. The publisher was unmoved by my assertion that, at the same age, I was required to be able to spell and define words like 'sinecure'. Does this matter? I think so. Put simply, we think in language. If there isn't a word for something, or that word is not in our vocabulary, it impairs our ability to know – and also to communicate. Which is one of the reasons I have had so much joy (*nuannapoq* even . . .) with the Inuit words in this book.

So what do you do when your book is too quiet and too literary for the current market? There seemed to be three options: 1, lie down and die (only I'm not very good at that); 2, lie down and die (I seriously considered it); 3, put up or shut up.

I decided on 3 and began researching crowd-funding platforms. What if I could reach a whole new community? A cross section of people who cared about children's literature and also about the planet? I started to put together a Kickstarter campaign. And thanks to people who know considerably more about social media than I do (thank you Candy Gourlay, thank you S. F. Said) word began to get out. The book you're holding in your hands is the result of that power – people power. And also of trust. People trusted me. (That was – and remains to me – pretty humbling). And perhaps it's also the face of a brave new world where publishing (and what can be successfully published) is gradually, but fundamentally, changing. Where we might be looking be looking, say, at a new – international – version of the 18th-century subscription model?

But let's return to the heroes of this particular story. The people listed below who actually made this project happen: my family; my friends; people from the world of children's books (editors, agents, translators, writers); librarians; teachers; environmentalists (workers, activists, writers, advisors to government); musicians, composers, theatre-makers, film-makers, the odd lawyer, a totally non-demonic banker and also names that will be as unfamiliar to you as they were to me – that incredible band of generous strangers from all over the world who took a risk on me. I thank each and every one:

ACHUKA; Nina Allan; Noga Applebaum; Laura Atkins; Adam Baghdadi; Helen and John Barnes; Philip Bartle; Mandy Beall; Susan Benn; Don Black; Rebecca Boey; Jilly Bond; P. S. Brooks; Mark Burgess; Tom Burke; Christopher Burn; Tim Burnett; Alex Burton-Keeble; C. J. Busby; Moira Butterfield; Dawn Casey; Liz Casey; Kops Chow; Miss Rachael Claridge; Jo Clark; Catherine Coe; Conville and Walsh; James Cooney; Chris Cooper; Liz Cross; Linda Daunter; Sue Downie; Alan Durant; Ros Edmonds and family; Daniela Essart; Felix Faber; Robert Faber & Kim Pickin; Ian & Sarah Farringdon; Tia Fisher; Janet Foxley; Philip Franks; GD; Vanessa Gebbie; Debra Goodman; Paulette Gordon-Stewart; Candy Gourlay; Lynda Graham; Maxine Gully; Daniel Hahn; Jan Hall; Henny; Lucy Hooberman; Deborah Holmes; Monica B. Holmes; Paul Hudson; Alexandra Jackson Kay; Beverley Johnson; Siân Jones; Anne Kavanagh; Simon Kenny; Liz King-Smith; Ann Kronbergs; Sharada Laidlay; Joost Landgraf; Katherine Langrish; Trisha Lee; Lennhoff Family; Bronagh Liddicoat; Jen Lunn; Will Mabbitt; Kristin Mason; Geraldine McCaughrean; Katharine McEwen; Noella Mingo; Jonathan Monk; Nicola Morgan; Lucinda Morrison; Adele Moss; Miriam Moss; Charlotte Mulliner; Beverley Naidoo; Katie Naylor; Valerie Niblett; Stine Nilsen; Jude Obermüller; Mary Parker; Guy Parker-Rees; Esmé Patey-Ford; Deborah Perkin; Lesley Parr; Clare Paterson; Lucy Pearce, Womancraft Publishing; Lola Perrin; Julie Pike; Fabrice Piwnica; Cindy Polemis; Pop Up Projects CIC; Emily Precious; Jacquie Pritchard; Phil Pritchard; Richard; James Riley; Charlotte Rivington; Amy Rogers; Frances Rose; Martin and George Rose; Mandy Rutter; S. F. Said; Nikki Sheehan; Jo Sheldon; Colin Singer;

Jackie Singer; Janet Singer and Alan Edwards; Stephanie Singer; Molly Singer-Kingsmith; Edmund Singer-Kingsmith; Roland Singer-Kingsmith; Francesca Singer Smith and Mr Tom Ince, Esq.; Arthur Slade; Shelley Souza; Kay Stephan; Roger Stevens; Gloria Sullivan; Jan Sullivan-Chalmers; Luke Temple; Sarah Towle; Jaime Unson; Eleanor Updale; Janet Waddicor; Jenny Waldman; Sue Wallman; Hope Estella Whitmore; Rupert Widdicombe; Caroline Williams; Claire Williams; Nigel Wilson; Debbie Wiseman.

People on (and off . . .) this list put in different amounts of money. Many put in more than they could afford. One person put in an insane amount of money. He thought I wouldn't know, he thought donations were anonymous. Bad luck, PG!

Some people gave me other things too – things that money can't buy. Writers Dawn Casey and Bille Eltringham gave me hope as well as detailed feedback on the manuscript. Michael Rosen (who I bumped into at the Brighton Festival) gave me gracious permission to quote from *I'm Going on a Bear Hunt* – a total favourite in our family as well as in Cameron's. Agent Clare Conville read with her perceptive, critical eye, as always. Tolly Rose provided photographs of lavatories and doors into other universes. Georgie Gadian, *'Aged 11 (nearly 12)'* – her brackets (true say!)– promised trenchant feedback on the story – but stopped scribbling after page 20 when she got 'carried away with reading'. That's the nicest sort of feedback, Georgie! Last but by no means least is Karen Jones' class of cinquièmes at the bi-lingual ASEICA school in Nice who graded my re-write *Mention Très Bien*.

So. Finally.

Target reached. Book ready.

Production about to begin.

And then, in the midst of all the excitement, I have a Massive Loss of Confidence.

This happens to writers. Some days we are bullish. We have to be in order to get up and go to our desks and work there in silence for seven hours a day with no one to praise (or blame) us but ourselves. Sometimes we are not quite so bullish. The days when, for instance, we allow ourselves to feel overwhelmed by the lack of interest from the people at the other end of the publishing food chain – the ones with the water-coolers and the regular monthly salaries – and . . . and . . . and . . . here I am busy getting myself in a knot because, actually . . .

. . . soon there will be real books –

. . . and Real People will read them –

. . . and what if I've written a turkey, after all?

My head is hurting. I can't work. I take myself off to Waterstones and I'm just sitting there with my cup of tea and Someone Else's Book (oh blessed relief), when this vandal comes in and starts drawing on the walls. He says his name is Chris and he's allowed. The pictures are quite good. In fact they're very good. Which is not surprising on account of the fact that he turns out to be the illustrator Chris Riddell, newly appointed UK Children's Laureate.

Anyway, we fall into conversation and Chris asks what I'm currently working on and I tell him about *Island* and also do some DGB (Doom, Gloom and Bitching) about the current state of children's publishing and he says suddenly – I'd like to do a few illustrations for your book. And I think, the coffee's well gone to his head. But the next day, on my Facebook page these appear:

And he's SERIOUS.

And I send him the book and a little while later he writes me: *Just finished reading your beautiful text and am now rather in love with 'Island'*. And after everything that has gone on, you will understand why this makes me cry.

Chris has lots of other work to do – some Laureate work, the small matter of a Neil Gaiman book to illustrate . . . but he makes time for *Island* and even posts about it.

And then he sends me the real pictures. The ones you see in the book. Well – I don't think I have to add anything to them. Except – perhaps – thank you, Chris. Thank you SO much.

Although, for the record, you should know that Chris is donating his share of any proceeds to Greenpeace. Which just shows you, if you needed any further evidence, what sort of man he is.

And finally we have Charles Boyle and Trevor Wilson. Charles is a writer. I first spotted him writing (poetry) at his desk in the dull office we shared in our early twenties. He now runs the tiny, award-winning, independent press CB editions, which he still operates single-handedly from his front room. Charles is a tireless champion of homeless literature: poetry, short fiction, translations, the lost and the forgotten. It was Charles who first offered to take *Island* under his wing. And it's Trevor, of Caboodle Books, who has put in the extra money to extend the print run so there will be books in bookshops and available to share in schools. Trevor also runs Authors Abroad and, with this hat on, he will help put me in those schools so the discussion can finally start with the really important people – the children.

And who made that happen?

YOU.

In gratitude and affection –

Nicky Singer
September 2015

Nicky Singer www.nickysinger.co.uk
Chris Riddell www.chrisriddell.co.uk
Greenpeace www.greenpeace.org.uk
Charles Boyle www.cbeditions.com
Trevor Wilson www.authorsabroad.com

RESOURCES

There are many wonderful websites where you can find out more about the impact human activity is having on the Arctic and the creatures that live there. One of my favourites is www.dontbeabuckethead.org. On this website you can hear marine mammal sounds and songs (which are amazing) and see the impact (interactive video) of man-made noise on different Arctic creatures. As dontbeabuckethead puts it: *Man-made noise affects sea creatures like putting a bucket on your head. When they can't hear, they can't live.*

Or as Inuluk puts it: *If whale had named the planet he would have called it not Planet Earth but Planet Sea. So little earth. So much sea.*

Dreaming
of a
Distant
ISLAND
GUIDED BY
INUIT
SPIRITS
SUNDAY
12TH JULY